Specters Anonymous

by

PHIL BUDAHN

Rosetta had entered the here-after with sensible shoes, a tweed suit and the squint of one who felt death was no excuse for bad posture.

"Perhaps as a topic for tonight's gathering," Rosetta said, "I would like to suggest *thanks-a-bunch*."

Among the spooks in the circle of chairs, a few eyeballs rolled back. Some kept spinning.

"What's that about?" I heard a newbie whisper behind me.

Over my shoulder I whispered, "*Thanks-a-bunch* is recovery-speak for *Boy, I'm really glad I don't have to trim my toenails anymore.*"

"Ahh!"

I took a closer look at the newcomers. A lean, young woman perched above a folding metal chair with a knee tucked under her chin. She had one hand clamped tightly over her mouth as though she might say something silly if she weren't careful. Another young woman looked to be the love child of Darth Vader and Elvira Mistress of the Dark. And a kid, somewhere in his late teens, glowered at everyone. His sleeves were rolled up so no one could miss the tattoos on his arms or fail to appreciate what a bad customer he was.

Me, I wasn't impressed. I've had a few twenty-four hours of post-mortality. I can pick out a newbie who is still jittery from his last taste of fresh air and can't wait for another shot of sunlight.

Cal caught my eye. Cal was my sponsor, which, according to him, gives him the right to run my afterlife. He arched an eyebrow meaningfully, looked at the newbie with the tats and nodded at me. So now I knew which train he wanted me to jump on three seconds before the wreck; I pretended not to see him. He arched the other brow. I pretended harder. He arched both eyebrows.

Cool as a rat in a jar of formaldehyde, I looked at him and shook my head.

Cal folded his arms and closed his eyes. Making a show of being beyond it all, of having *resigned from the shouting match*, to use a phrase from our literature. Still, his features blurred as he was enveloped in a sheet of – what would pass in the daylight world for – steam.

Did I mention this was a smoking meeting?

Fortunately for the state of my transcendence, during that drama I missed Darleen's tale about how she had come to the group and how things got better once she realized she was powerless over life. Not that I had an attitude about the old-timers who'd been around long enough to actually remember what they were doing before they were shoved through the great turnstile of fate into happily-ever-after. Darleen was our resident pixie: none of her glasses was ever half-empty, three-quarters empty or even 99.95 percent empty.

Thing is, if I heard one more time about Darleen trying to pull that thin blue hospital blanket over her neck because she was cold and her pale fingers passed right through the fabric, I was going to start throwing things. And that, for a member of Specters Anonymous, is almost as dangerous as hanging around a tanning salon.

Darleen ended with the admission there's no cure for being in post-life, only a nightly reprieve from the alternatives so long as we're diligent in our program. On that note, she sighed. A silence descended on the circle of chairs, the Uber-quiet that comes when a roomful of dead people realize no one can think of anything to say.

"I'm Elizabeth Hannity. And I'm a happy specter."

Every face turned to Mrs. Hannity with a smile. Mrs. Hannity was every-body's grandmother. White-haired, soft-spoken, dimple-cheeked, the matron of our group and one of its pillars, although she had some gaps in her understanding of recovery.

"I think a lot about *thanks-a-bunch*," she said, "and I find it helps to make a list. It's in my mind, of course — that list — owing to the problems I have these nights with arthritis and my bad eyesight and not having a physical form that can hold a pencil. My list has everything I have to be thankful for. Maybe you would find it useful."

She looked around the group with sparkling gray eyes before continuing. "Let's see what I can remember. I can honestly say, *thanks-a-bunch* for not having any more dishes to wash. Or finding some teenager in the neighborhood — wherever that may be — to rake the leaves in the fall. Or not needing to change a kitty-litter box. Or worrying about the right time to plant my tomatoes. Or programming the *whatschamadoodle* that records movies on TV."

She went on in this vein, and by the time she finished, I was ready to shoot myself. Even though it would be wasted effort. Or jump off a bridge, with results that come in the *ditto* category.

"I'm Ralph. And I'm a carcass," I chimed, to a pained smile from Rosetta. "I've had problems with *thanks-a-bunch*. Not that I want to go back to any place that has mosquitoes, but struggling with *thanks-a-bunch* has shaken my transcendence at times. For example, I've had to accept not having body odor."

"That's not what they say at Forest Lawn," Hank muttered.

I plunged ahead, "I had to be thankful for not thinking about what to wear or when to brush my teeth. Not paying taxes and not worrying whether my clothes are a little nerdy — that's been hard to take. And knowing I'll never stand next to a woman on a crowded bus who's wearing enough perfume to asphyxiate a skunk. I'm still working on being thankful for that one."

When I finished, Rosetta sputtered and stammered. Everyone started talking at once. Half the spooks in the room wanted to show they were cleverer than I, while the other half insisted that death was no laughing matter. Rosetta called on Fast Eddie, who could be counted on every week to take us through his final seven minutes with a pulse as he tried to dust the Harvard classics on the top shelf of the reference section in a library.

Fast Eddie was just showing off, as usual. He remembers.

After thirty minutes, like every other 12-step program on two planes of existence, we had half-time. In the first life, half-time was a pause in the discussion to grab a quick cigarette, visit the restroom, refill a coffee mug or toss a buck into the wicker basket that circled the room for donations.

Not one of these things affected us, owing to a certain reluctance of the laws of physics to apply to spooks, but we still had half-time. Futility is a hard thing to give up.

Hank and I stepped outside. He has ectoplasm the color of chocolate milk and a small pigtail at the back of his head. Even Rosetta and Mrs. Hannity have their knees go weak when Hank's at a meeting, but, more than any other spook I know, he thinks that transcendence is a matter of putting your head down and shoving your way forward.

Hank and I may or may not be friends. We're still working that out, but we have this half-time routine every night. We step outside at half-time because somebody's gotta.

The newbie who might be Darth Vader's off-spring joined us.

"Hey," she said.

"Hey," I replied. Yeah, zippy dialogue comes naturally to me.

"My name's Gilda," she said, then, not quite making it a question, she asked, "Did you mean what you said in there? About not buying any of that *thanks-a-bunch* stuff."

I'd already blanked out most of my rant. Struggling to recall the details, I shuddered. "You know I was exaggerating, right? Comic effect and all that."

"So you were lying." She fixed on me a gaze that could have been locked down with bolts and a lug wrench. "We're really supposed to be thrilled to be here."

Need I mention the first seventeen answers that came to mind were flippant? But Gilda was a new-arrival, and newbies are what the program is all about. I didn't need Cal to tell me this, although he did incessantly.

"I don't have to like something to need it. I don't even have to understand it," I said. "A while back, for example, a spook talked at a meeting about her honeymoon. The word went through me like lightning. Honeymoon. I can't explain it, but it's been driving me nuts ever since, and all of that's probably good for me. For my transcendence."

Gilda's look was the equivalent of three physicals and a dental check-up. Without another word, she went back through the door, nodding thoughtfully.

"That spook was putty in your hands," Hank said.

When we returned to our gray metal chairs, Rosetta was fidgety. Having your torso and limbs in a box six feet under the grass doesn't necessarily mean you're relaxed about wasting time.

"Before we resume our sharing of personal experiences, does anyone have anything they would like to discuss for the good of the group?" Rosetta asked. Usually, this was a chance for the mathematically inclined to tell us how many days, months, years, decades or centuries they have of posthumous recovery.

The kid with the tats and the attitude raised his hand. "Yeah, I'd like to know if anyone here has run across Tommy Squires. Passed on a couple months ago. Trying to break into professional auto racing."

The kid got a half-dozen "Nopes," a few more shaken heads and plenty of blank stares from the newbies along the wall.

Cal crossed his arms. "Do you want to tell us your name?"

"Yeah, sure. Fergus. Just Fergus."

"Welcome, Fergus," several of us murmured.

Fergus was quite moved. In fact, he loitered about a half-second and, receiving no information on the where-abouts of Tommy Squires, moved right through the door.

"Thanks for nothing," he muttered to himself as he passed me.

Cal caught my eye with a look that was chillier than midnight at the South Pole.

Ever think that post-respiration will be a time with nothing else to lose? Then you haven't spent five minutes in a small room with Cal when the old boy is having control issues. I gave him my sweetest smile and followed Fergus through the door.

I'm going to take an intuitive leap here by guessing that a high percentage of the folks who've stuck with me this far in the narration are starting to foam at the mouth. They want to get to the mechanics of the afterlife. Are we reunited with our families? Do we *have to be* reunited? Can we hang out with Elizabeth

CHAPTER Two

f happily-ever-after should strike you as a little dull, remember there's one sure way to get the ectoplasm flowing. Just ask, ever so naively in your next meeting of Specters Anonymous, about what happens *after* the afterlife. Then duck.

The religionists have the big light. The nihilists have the big nothing. And the free-thinkers are reserving the right to make a commitment at the last nano-second.

I'm partial to the free-thinkers. I'll stumble along until I have enough information to see – as it were – the light.

But when a beacon blazed at me as though my nose were a couple of inches from the sun, I felt silly being a skeptic. I could practically feel those photons peeling away my ectoplasm; in no time, I was going to be smaller than a gnat's shadow.

A thunderous, imperial voice resonated again from the brightness: "Come to the light. Come."

I spread my arms to the heavens. I was clean. I was pure. I was going home. "I'm coming," I screamed. "I'm coming."

And God replied, "What the bloody hell? Shut that damn thing off."

And darkness filled the void. Followed shortly by pin-pricks of light as cigarettes were lit across the face of the deep.

So there I was, woozy from a couple gazillion candlelights of illumination, watching a guy chomp on a month-old cigar as he unscrewed a panel on the side of a darkened searchlight that was still aimed down the street. Behind him in the shadows, a crowd of people came alive: everyone began talking at once.

A lone figure separated from the group beside the searchlights and walked slowly toward me. He was lean and business-like, possibly a lawyer, at least an MBA holder. In his hand was something the size of a small melon. I shuddered. Sure, spooks are supposed to be invulnerable to physical objects. But where's that written down? And does it come with a guarantee that there's not some kind of rock out there, say, the afterlife's version of Kryptonite, that can smash my ectoplasmic brain into sludge?

We still had a Tosser on the loose, so I started inching toward the corner of the old house. Maybe I'd play with the Tossers some other night.

But the guy veered toward a couple of women standing in front of the searchlight. "Just a little touch-up," he said, and dabbed the rock – actually, a powder-puff – on the forehead of a woman who was tall and thin and dressed in a flowing white gown.

Last week at a meeting, Fast Eddie suspended his usual tale about being killed by the Harvard classics long enough to say that he'd seen a camera crew and dozens of people by the old Davis mansion. Fast Eddie said we should expect a newbie or two soon: only a photogenic auto wreck could drag the Eyewitness News Team and so many spectators to a deserted section of downtown after the 11 p.m. broadcast.

Old Eddie, it turned out, was miles off target. Not a news team, but a Hollywood film-crew.

"Thank you, Samuel," the actress said in husky syllables. The guy nodded with the solemnity befitting one who had just been knighted by a monarch, then turned away.

The second woman stepped forward. "Hey, wait a minute. What about me?"

Samuel kept going.

The second woman was smaller, younger and blonder than the star. I liked the way she was put together, although I'm beyond worldly superficiality, all that flutter and flimflam.

Ahem. Yes, most definitely.

"Angelica."

Again, the voice of God, who, on closer inspection, had a clipboard in his hand, a paunch the size of a late-term pregnancy, a toupee that would frighten even the folks on my side of the Great Divide, and an air of hauteur that must make the flies feel honored to land on his pasty butt.

"Angelica, darling, could you come here a sec? I want your opinion on the fabric for your costume in the cemetery scene."

Angelica, the tall one, glided toward the director. Leaving the little actress standing in the middle of the street with her hands on her hips. If looks could kill, Richmond, Virginia, would be getting a dramatic expansion of my favorite recovery program.

Unfortunately, I didn't have the time to enjoy the drama. Sunrise would be here sooner than anyone wanted and I had to report to Cal about Fergus. And about the Tosser. Cal would want to know about that. Although I can't swear that Fergus threw the rock at the house, I had my suspicions.

The next thing I knew, I was flying through the air. Not from some paranormal mode of transportation. But because someone in the afterlife ran into my back hard enough to knock me to the ground.

My face and hands met the concrete and kept on going. Who says death doesn't have its pluses? When I drifted back up to street-level and rolled over, I found myself looking at the little actress.

"I am so sorry," she gushed. "Are you okay? You landed so hard it looked like you fell right through the road." She knelt beside me, placed a hand on my chest.

"Don't move. They say you're not supposed to move when you've had a bad fall. Not until the paramedics say you're alright."

I wished I were someplace else. But I wasn't. I was where I was. And there was no way I could scramble or squirm around the moment that was coming.

As calmly as I could manage, I said, "What's your name?"

"Margie."

"Would you do something for me, Margie? Would you call for the paramedics?"

"Of course, yes." For a moment, she pressed her hands to both cheeks, and I wondered why I couldn't have met this woman six months before I got here. She said, "What am I thinking? Sure, call the paramedics."

Margie rose on her knees, swung back toward the film-crew and shouted: "Please call an ambulance. Somebody, please. This man's hurt. He needs professional help." I didn't take my eyes off her face. "Is someone calling the paramedics?"

"I can't tell. I don't think so."

"Why not?"

"Hey, there," Margie shouted again. "This has gone far enough. I need help. This is serious. Somebody please get an ambulance."

She had a nice face, not as striking perhaps as Angelica. The sort of face that people used to call *fresh-scrubbed*. That you could imagine getting prettier and softer when she became a mother, then a grandmother.

I shook off the thought about grandmothers. I had a job to do, and whether I wanted to or not, I had to finish it.

"What do you mean about things *going far enough?*" I asked.

"Some silly game. Nobody will give me the time of day. It's as though I'm not here."

I asked, "Is this happening only with these people, the film crew? What about the hotel where you slept last night? The restaurant where you ate today?"

"Hmmm. Funny. I can't remember where I slept last night. Did I eat today? I don't seem to remember that, either. Maybe that explains why I've been out of sorts lately. Just stepping into that searchlight beam made me woozy."

I took her hand. It'd been a long time since I'd felt a hand outside a 12-step meeting. "Margie, there's something you have to know. I don't expect you to understand it all at once. But it will explain some of the things you've been noticing lately."

In a shot, Margie was on her feet. Fear and a smidgen of anger flashed across that wonderful face.

"What are those people doing about the paramedics?" she said. "I tell you, you just can't count on people the way you used to. If it's important, you've got to do it yourself."

"Margie."

But Margie was heading back to the film-crew. She may have wobbled through a cart of coffee pots and donuts: the searchlight came on again for a moment and scrambled my vision. Less fuzzy was the way she apologized to the guy who was pushing the cart, and the fact that he continued on as though she weren't there.

As I watched her go, I bit my lower lip. One of Cal's favorite sayings is: *You can lead a corpse to the cemetery, but you can't convince him it's his party*. Everyone steps beyond the veil with a certain amount of bewilderment and skepticism — heck, Specters Anonymous wouldn't exist if it were a clear, effortless transition — yet, I found myself wishing I'd known Margie when a party was really a party.

On the porch of the derelict house on the corner stood a little guy in a wrinkled black suit, white shirt with ruffles down the front and a narrow black tie. His moustache was pencil thin, his hair mussed-up and his eyes had a haunted quality.

Slowly, he raised a hand. "Quoth the raven, *Nevermore*."

"Yeah, yeah. Whatever."

CHAPTER

A s you might have gathered from my tale about Margie, my current home isn't called *The Great Divide* for nothing. Although the physical world is the stage, as it were, for the spectral dimension, the temporarily breathing and the permanent non-breathers don't have much to do with each other, and when we do, there's usually some rule, tradition, aphorism or nugget from my recovery program that tells us to quit doing that right now.

My tally for a full night of specterhood came down to: A) two new arrivals – Fergus and Margie – whom I couldn't help, B) a third newbie, Gilda, who was too weird for me to want to help, C) a Tosser I couldn't locate, and D-Q) Edgar Allen Poe was back in my afterlife. It was time to call it a night.

At that time, I parked my ectoplasm in a shack on Belle Island. I whispered, "Beam me up, Scotty," and I was there. The narrow stretch of the James River that separated the island from the downtown glistened from the street lamps. That glow from the city was strong enough to make me itch all over, but I'll admit it was pretty.

All I wanted, at this point, was to crawl into my bucket inside the shack and have a good day's rest.

Wwwrraaaaakk!

A pebble rolled down the shack's sloping tin roof, sounding like the percussion section of a run-away symphony orchestra. I scanned the scraggly bushes on either side of the shack. Cal has given me words of advice for every possible event under the moon – a couple of which I can remember in a pinch – but nothing pops into my mind involving pursuit by Tossers.

"You're not going to frighten me," I called out. "Fergus! Do you hear me?"

Somewhere in the darkness, the Tosser said, "Hmmm."

A Tosser hmmmed?

Through the fractured planks of the shack's door stepped a black boot, followed by a leg sheathed in black hose, a black skirt, purple fingernails, a black leather jacket over a black blouse, black eyeliner, black hair. Everything that wasn't black or purple was chalky white. Except for the lips. They were as red as fresh cherries.

A light – a shielded, low-wattage light with a rheostat at its dimmest setting – came on in my head. "You were at the meeting tonight."

"Yeah."

Gilda looked at the ground when she moved, and I could believe she was worried about tripping over something, which doesn't happen to the residents of happily-ever-after.

"Did you do that with the rock?" I asked.

"Yeah. I tried to knock, but my hand kept going through the wood. Bummer."

Fancy that. A dead Goth with some sense of courtesy.

"Yeah, wood does that to us these nights. But the stuff with the rocks – not recommended in our 12-step program." I tried to smile encouragingly. "What brings you here?"

"We were talking about *thanks-a-bunch* at the meeting. Do you remember that?"

"Sure." I was beginning to get the idea that Gilda had traveled all the way from the material world to the spirit world without leaving her own planet. "Is there something you're having trouble saying *thanks-a-bunch* for?"

Those possum eyes fixed on me. "I don't like being someplace where so many other people are wearing black. Have these people run out of imagination? *puh-LEEES.*"

I looked at her and wondered what Cal would say if he were here. Or Jesus Christ. Or Sigmund Freud. Or Susan B. Anthony.

The best I could do was: "The sun will be up soon. We've got to get some rest. See you later tonight."

"At the meeting?" she said. "Same time, same place?"

"That's the ticket."

I slipped through the shack's flimsy door. My bucket was a galvanized classic model, with a roll of green tar paper stretched over the top and a couple cans of paint weighing down the tar paper, all stuffed under a work-bench. It wasn't pretty, but it was light-proof.

"Knock, knock."

"Who's there?"

"Gilda."

"Gilda who?"

"Gilda who just wants to tell you something about honeymoons."

I stuck my head through the door, peeved at myself for having revealed anything personal to a newbie. An altered state of existence did enough to my thought processes, thank you very much, without adding commentary from a bewildered and frightened newcomer. Listening to one of them can add layers of complexity to the phrase *taking a shot in the dark*.

Steam must have been leaking out of my ears. "What did you just remember?"

"I remember seeing an old-time television show. It was called *The Honeymooners*."

"Fancy that." No cathedral bells were ringing. Not even a tinkling dinner bell. "Thanks for mentioning it."

I was pulling my head through the planks when Gilda added: "One of the characters in that show. His name was Ralph, too."

My first recollection of post-mortality was standing in a fog bank that oozed from the ground in a dim corridor. I was part of a crowd of people with stunned looks, whose fingers kept straying to their own necks and wrists to check again for a pulse. Eventually, I worked my way to the head of the line and stood in front of a rickety table, where I was handed a pencil stub by a bald guy in a checkered bow tie and a dark sweater whose sleeves barely covered his wrists.

"Sign the register," he said.

I took one look and realized that something was profoundly wrong. "I . . . I don't remember my name."

"That's why you're signing, buddy. Right there. Put your name down."

"But I really don't have a clue."

Carefully, he set his hands on the thick register and intertwined his fingers. I sensed a great mass of humanity behind me, shuffling their feet and muttering about the hold-up.

"Just sign," the man said.

I was aware of my hand moving, but I wasn't sure what I was doing until I dropped the pencil, took a half-step back, and ogled the letters scratched onto the page. Crude, irregular but clear:

Ralph.

"Is that my name?" I asked.

"Signed, sealed and delivered," was his reply. "Now, take that door," he added, jabbing a thumb over his shoulder.

"Where does it go?"

"We aren't going to know that until you get there. Now, off you go."

"Yeah, off I go."

Gilda ended up spending the night in a rusty paint can in my shack because she wasn't sure she could find a safe, dark place before sun-up. She was checking her nails the next evening when I squeezed out of my bucket.

"Looks like someone slept on his head" was her greeting.

Which is further proof that the here-after isn't a gender-free zone. I could drift into Hank's place with my severed head tucked under an arm, and he'll ask if I saw the game last night. But a spook of the female persuasion will feel comfortable commenting on my appearance or my emotional afterlife within minutes of meeting me for the first time.

It just goes to show that you can take the spirit out of the woman, but you'll never get the woman out of the spirit.

"Let me guess," was my counter-greeting. "You always welcome the twilight by whistling a cheerful tune."

"Don't be ghastly," the black-clad spectral Goth said. "There's only one way to give the evening a proper start."

She looked at me. I looked at her. A searchlight placed inches from my head couldn't force a reaction from me.

Still, Gilda snapped her purple-nailed fingers and said, "That's right. Pecan pancakes and fresh blueberries."

I shuddered.

Soon, we were in a booth of the waffle house near the campus. Gilda practically sat in the lap of a sunshiner who was going through a stack of pancakes like a starving horse. I was wedged into the corner because the guy's girlfriend seemed to think a fork was some sort of communications device needed to let the world know when she was making an important point. Which happened every third syllable.

I'm beyond being harmed by a reckless fork, but old habits die hard. I can concentrate better without sharp metal jabbing the air at eye-level.

Gilda twirled a finger in the syrup on the guy's plate without making a ripple. Nary a drop was lost as she studied her finger, mostly because her finger was bone dry, to use an unfortunate phrase. Then she sucked on her finger as though she could taste anything if anything were there.

"Well," she said, catching my look. "You can't blame a girl for trying. Someday I intend to get lucky."

"You and a few billion other spooks."

But the fact is that sometimes we do get lucky. We can interact with the material world safely for a short time and in little ways — like nudging a feather off a desk — although I haven't figured out that trick yet. Emphasis here is upon *safely*. No holds are barred whenever one of us wants to go the way of the Tossers.

I've asked Cal to explain this. He tells me to stay out of the sunshine.

Gilda waited until the guy who couldn't see her wasn't looking at his food before sticking a finger he couldn't see into the syrup on his plate, and I wondered which deceased brain cell of mine thought I should engage this Goth in a serious conversation. But last night's encounter with the spotlight, plus Gilda's revelation about a television show called *Honeymooners* and a character named Ralph had rattled me, big time.

"Can you remember anything about that TV show?" I asked.

"Just the name and the fat guy called Ralph." She had difficulty taking her eyes off our booth-mate's plate. "You think it's important?"

"Maybe not, but it does tie together two mysteries — my name and the way I react when someone says *honeymoon*."

"Maybe in your first life, you had a honeymoon with someone named Ralph."

"Naw, I still remember what hormones are like. That can't be it."

"So, you're making progress. You ought to be dancing on the ceiling. Why so glum?"

"I fell off the hearse last night." I shook my head. "My recovery is in ruins."

Gilda wrinkled her nose. "Do you mean you want to go back to being a breather?"

"No. . . . Yes. . . . I don't know." I watched the young woman who shared our booth try to spear a runny scrambled egg. "I got in the beam of a spotlight."

Gilda studied the tip of her dry finger, shrugged, and examined the little metal beaker of syrup from which the young man had saturated his pancakes with sweet liquid.

"Did you intend to go into a spotlight?" she asked, more interested in the syrup than in me.

"No, I didn't know it was there. I was pretty surprised when it came on."

"Did you try to leave it?"

"There wasn't time. It turned off before I realized what was happening."

She stopped her examination of the syrup. Something told me a bombshell was about to come fizzing in my direction. With great indifference, she asked, "Did you enjoy it?"

The question surprised me. As did my answer. "Not a bit. Not for a second."

"There you go." Her eyes lit up, and I wondered what she would look like liberated from her eyeliner, butterfly eyelashes and pasty powder.

No stumblies for me. Not with the searchlight. A stumbling specter would have hurled himself at that mega-watt monster and hugged it for all it was worth. Getting drunk on the feeling that we can go back to the world, to our pre-decedent existence.

Cal being Cal, and especially Cal being my 12-step sponsor, would have to hear about the searchlight from my own lips. But I was no longer terrified that he was going to wheedle me and coax me with generous dollops of shame and the occasional threat, until I raised my hand at a meeting when they asked if anyone was within his first thirty years of transcendence.

This Gilda kid was alright.

As our booth-mates left to wander, oh, so casually, out the back door before the check arrived, Gilda winked at me and said, "Want to try a little experiment?"

"Does it involve teaching free-loaders the importance of paying their bills?"

"Better," Gilda replied. "It involves blueberries."

Her plan was based upon the fact that a spook couldn't interact with materiality, not, at least, in the *normal* order of abnormal things. No touching people or physical objects, with the exception of rocks and stones (I can't explain that one, either), and no communication with breathers via verbal, written, digital or telepathic means (with enough exceptions to shove a haunted house through). However, we were perfectly able to touch and communicate with each other.

There is, after all, a difference between death and solitary confinement.

Gilda wanted to pick up a single blueberry smothered in syrup from the plate of pancakes. We both knew that wasn't going to happen: when she tried, her fingers slipped through the little round pod like a bag of sand through a pool of water. But, since she could touch me, didn't that mean that the two of us, dedicating a single digit each to the task and working in coordination, should be able to pick up a blueberry if we came on it like a tweezers?

Somewhere there was a flaw in her logic, but I was still so grateful for her help getting out of the doldrums over the spotlight, that I agreed to try.

Scrunching down by the booth, my eyes inches from the plate and the single, slippery, coal-black prize, I reconnoitered my objective. Then, like the prow of a sailing ship breasting through the fog, my trigger finger uncurled from my fist. I leaned closer: this was going to be a highly delicate maneuver.

A waitress hollered an order for BLTs, light on the cow; a table of under-grads grew giggly halfway through their first pitcher of beer; and a German shepherd glanced in the front window, caught my eye, and ran off whimpering.

Through the glass, I could see passing on the other side of the street, Fergus, my suspected Tosser from last night.

CHAPTER

ight was spreading from the east like a stain of black ink spilled on the sky when I shot through the deli's door after Fergus. I'm not revealing any state secrets if I point out that twilight is a favorite time for newbies. Some old-timers, too, are partial to the fuzzy middle-ground between night and day, especially if they're still trying to convince themselves that a funeral, a casket and weeping relatives aren't conclusive proof of their own demise.

Which explains why Fergus had to weave his way through specters lining the sidewalks of Broad Street and snaking down the side-streets. Picture the crowd watching a Macy's parade, then shift the venue from New York to Purgatory. Now you see what I mean.

In a handful of minutes between full sunset and the time the street lights come on, these wannabe-rebreathers can pretend that nothing has changed. They can get as close to the sunlight as they dare. I saw twin sisters make-believe they were balancing on the edge of the curb like tight-rope walkers. The poor kids were so new to this side of forever their feet kept sinking into the concrete.

An elderly couple walked arm-in-arm, taking in the cool air. A middle-aged fellow with one of the few beer bellies I've seen on a spook, crouched against a building in the deep shadow under an awning. I didn't need a biography to know the guy with the paunch tried to take a stroll outside this afternoon.

A soldier with haunted eyes gripped my arm and asked, "How do I get to Arlington National Cemetery from here?"

"You'll have to die again, soldier," I replied.

On the other side of Broad, Rosetta waved. She started across the street toward me, but hopped back to the sidewalk when a taxi roared past. Guess I'm not the only one who still refuses to do the sorts of things that could have killed me. Rosetta shrugged, waved again with a plucky smile, and turned back to the crowd of specters.

Twilight was prime hunting for members of my recovery group like Rosetta who believe that new spooks would someday thank them for being forced into recognizing they're now daisy food.

Fergus was about twenty feet ahead of me now and plowing forward without side-stepping to avoid the breathers rushing home from their businesses and their shopping forays. When he reached the center of a block dominated by a boarded, ten-story brick monolith that once had been the downtown J.C. Penny's store, Fergus simply winked out of existence.

Or so it appeared. The only way to know for certain was to get to the same spot as soon as possible, hope that the conditions were fundamentally unchanged, and pray I wouldn't wake up someplace where mountains gnash against each other and fresh lava is the preferred beverage.

Ducking around a man with a cell-phone pressed to his ear, I reached the spot where Fergus had disappeared. Nothing. Traffic roared, newbies grinned in the dusk as though they'd never seen concrete before, and breathers taunted us with every exhalation of their puffing lungs.

I bobbed aside to avoid being drawn through a sunshiner with such luxurious rolls of fat I would despair of ever emerging out the other side. For the briefest moment, I felt a little woozy – and then I was somewhere else. Outside an old house. The leaves of a neighboring magnolia carpeted the ground with leathery scales layered over roots that heaved the sidewalk in a dozen places. Paint hung in flakes from the walls, although the porch had a freshly applied coat of yellow and blue; the windows were buried beneath decades of grime.

"Jeez, this is creepy even for us dead folks."

I jumped at the voice.

Gilda was standing beside me. Looking as though she didn't know I was there.

Then she noticed me.

"Why are you following me?" she snapped before I could open my mouth. "Don't think you can fool me. Just because you get somewhere first, it doesn't mean you're not a stalker."

I stammered and stuttered and abandoned all hope of stringing together a coherent sentence.

She swept through the fence to get a closer look at the house. A wind slithered through the leaves of the ancient magnolia. I waited for the crack of a rock landing on a roof or the rumble it made rolling down worn shingles.

"What are we doing here?" Gilda said.

"Remember the newbie at the meeting last night? The one who asked if anyone had seen a guy, then left early? I think he might have been a Tosser."

For the first time since I'd known her, Gilda's face took on a strange twitch. I think she was trying to smile.

"So that's what a Tosser looks like," she said. "What's the big deal? Chucking a few stones at your shack last night didn't do anything for me. Is there suppose to be some kind of a kick?"

I shrugged.

"Have you ever tried it?" she asked.

"No."

"Ever been tempted?"

"No."

She studied me. What is it about death that will change practically everything except that half-amused, half-judgmental look women give men?

This wasn't the moment to tell Gilda that my sponsor will get very cranky if he finds out that Fergus, a newbie he wanted me to help, turned out to be a Tosser, and that I hadn't even said, *Hi*, to the poor spook.

That twitchy, maybe-smile came to Gilda again. "You think the Tosser is inside? Maybe there's a casket in the basement where he goes during the daylight."

"Let's not get worked up over some silly old gravedigger's tale."

Next thing you know, Gilda was going to tell me that there really are haunted houses on this side of here-after, places that can scare the ectoplasm out of a specter. I was beginning to get a bad feeling about this Goth. For a newbie, she was entirely too much like an old-timer.

I glided to the front door, paused a moment for Gilda to catch up, then slid through the door.

The door had other plans. In fact, it knocked me on my butt. I didn't know whether to haul myself off the ground first or put my jaw back in place.

A remnant of the physical world had actually maintained its material characteristics in the spirit world.

I looked at Gilda. She said, "Maybe we should knock."

"Give me a sec."

Okay, this shouldn't be a big deal. I dealt with houses for my entire (first) life without any problem. So, a house is here physically, plain as night. It's not as though I don't know how to operate one.

"Just follow me," I said.

I went to the door, grabbed the knob — Wowee, I was actually touching something, just like the old days — turned the knob and pushed. With a squeal that had to have been the last gasp of a dying hinge, the door swung open. Inside was a living room with a couple of old sofas with poorly made covers, overflowing bookcases of cinderblocks and untreated planks, a small assortment of hard-backed chairs, and a coffee table whose best days hadn't come in the last two centuries.

"This could have been my old dorm room," Gilda said. "That is, if my old dorm room ever appeared in a Hollywood slasher movie."

I rapped the back of a chair. My knuckles made actual contact with wood to produce an audible sound (*knock, knock*), and I felt an amazing sensation pass up my arm that, if memory serves, was a kind of mild pain, that and a satisfying appreciation of the chair's solidity.

Gilda stepped on the cushions of a ratty sofa. She sank, but not because her immateriality failed to resonate on the same somatic plane as the sofa. She sank because the springs were shot.

"Hey, look at me," she said, laughing, as she bounded up and down on the divan, trampoline-fashion.

I laughed, too. Then I joined her on the other sofa. Up and down, down and up, sometimes coordinating our bounces, sometimes going like automobile pistons, we jumped. When I hit my head on the ceiling, the entire house rocked. We hooted. Gilda tried to leap high enough to hit the ceiling, too, and I heard her hair skim the plaster overhead with the hiss of a startled rattler.

That sinister, reptilian noise brought me back to — what passes these nights for — reality. I had followed a Tosser (whom Cal had always put in his list of the top ten threats to a successful transcendence) into a house that, for the first time in my limited experience beyond the pale, didn't act as if it were constructed of colored smoke. And I was becoming a nine-year-old during recess.

Was something wrong with this picture?

Gilda bounded upward. I reached across the coffee table and pulled her leg, bringing her down on the cushions on her butt. She grinned like a kid, but she looked away and covered her mouth and did everything but pull her leather jacket over her head to conceal the fact that she was having a good time.

"That was okay," she said. "We don't have to do it again." She paused, studied the floor. "Maybe one more time wouldn't hurt."

She scrambled to her knees on the cushion. Her look, as her fingers stroked the sofa's stained and tattered cover, was pure decadence. I doubt petting a mink coat ever brought such an expression of utter lasciviousness.

We're not here to pretend we're alive, Cal has told me a couple hundred times. *Anything that lets you ignore the situation is dangerous*. I'll confess to not understanding his advice until this moment.

"We better forget about the Tosser and get out of here." I glanced toward the front door. "We can come back later with Cal."

"So a sponsor is someone who holds your hand all the time." Gilda gave a few tentative, baby-sized bounces on the sofa cushion. "You can go get your sponsor, I'll be right here."

"I guess I'll stay, too."

"That a boy! Stand up to him."

"It's a little complicated," I answered. "I can't seem to find the door."

Gilda had cocked her arms behind her back and prepared for an epochal launch toward the ceiling, but she hesitated. "What do you mean?"

"I mean that the door has left since we came inside."

"Left?"

"Gone away. Evaporated. Is playing hide-and-seek."

"Nah, look it's just —" But when she scanned the dark wall behind her, she had to notice a shortage of exits. "Didn't we come down that hall?"

I nodded.

She dug her fists into her waist. George Patton would be a wimp next to this spook. "Let's be reasonable. We're dead, what can possibly happen to us?"

A large book – Herman Melville, I think – rose from the cinderblock shelves on the other side of the room, wavered slightly, then catapulted across the room at my head. Too many speeding cars passing harmlessly through my spectral body had dulled my reactions, but I managed to take only a glancing blow.

"Yeow. That smarts."

The next thing that rose from the bookshelves was a cinderblock. "Criminy," Gilda said as she dove over the back of the sofa: the cinderblock whooshed overhead, hit the wall with a thump that rattled teeth downtown, and burrowed into the plaster.

We made it to the dining room before the plastic cups, paper plates and plastic forks and spoons on the table began twitching like crickets rousing from a nightmare. We were out the swinging door into the kitchen when the contents of the dining room table launched.

"Back," Gilda said.

She dug in her heels and pushed me toward the swinging door before I could register that the drawers by the sink were rattling as though they were filled with steel dice. A drawer flew out of the counter and crashed on the floor, spilling enough cutlery for a slaughterhouse.

Gilda and I were back in the dining room when gleaming tips of steak knives began poking through the walls. A ceramic elephant wobbled on the floor, and I didn't see the necessity of studying the phenomenon longer to determine what was likely to happen. We scooted into the living room; my eyes fixed on the scabby wallpaper between the picture window and the rusted hooks on the wall for coats and hats, for this was the spot where the front door used to be.

History is the best predictor for the future, Ms. Krabitz, my least-favorite high school teacher used to say. Or, as applied to this situation: *A missing door is more likely to appear where it once was, than someplace it had never been.*

I lowered my shoulder, tucked my chin against my breast bone and tackled the wall, senses keen for any indication that the door was, in fact, exactly where we left it. I detected nothing but a solid wall and soon sprawled on the floor.

"Quit lying around, and do something," Gilda said.

"I'm open to suggestions."

I decided not to press the point when a hundred pound ceramic elephant hove into view around a corner and bobbled between the floor and the ceiling, as though deciding whether Gilda or I would look more interesting compacted to the size of a thimble.

I grabbed Gilda and dragged her to the staircase leading up. At the same time, in some back room of my mind, I registered the fact that getting from Point A to Point B now involved moving my legs, not the sort of tele-transportation that is the here-after's substitute for escalators.

As we pounded up the staircase, the railing gave way and crashed to the ground floor. Steps creaked and bowed downward and I was certain the rotten wood would give way entirely.

Ceramic Dumbo glided to the bottom of the stairs. I shouldn't have been surprised that, as it drifted up the steps in pursuit, it actually gathered speed. Nothing in this house was following the rules.

Gray light filtered down the hallway from a partly opened door. Gilda sprinted to it, with me trailing, desperately looking on both sides of the hall for pictures, tables, flower pots, anything to throw behind me to slow down Dumbo's ever-accelerating pursuit. The best weapons I could find were fragments of wallpaper the size of magnolia leaves and a handful of crumbly plaster.

Gilda was first in the room where an ashen glow diffused through a very large window. I slammed the door behind me. It fell off a hinge and leaned precariously against the door jamb. Through a crack in the wooden planks, I saw Dumbo arrive at the second-floor landing.

The window was of ancient design, with a brass handle in the center that would open two large sections of glass. Gilda hit the handle and swung open the pane on the right-hand, while I threw back the glass on the other side.

There were bars across the outside of the window, too narrow for us to squeeze through, and the only thing in the entire house that wasn't falling apart. My clever little mind told me that, being on the outside of the building, the bars would not abide by the same suspension of the rules of here-afterhood that applied to this freakish structure. That is, the bars might be spectral, not material.

I swung my fist at the dark metal and felt an excruciating spasm. No luck.

The ceramic elephant crashed through the door. I looked at Gilda and said, "Don't move. Do exactly what I tell you."

"And abandon all my values now?" She took up a firm, defiant stance.

"Be that way," I replied.

So after Dumbo hovered in the doorway a moment, as though choosing his target, then drifted back into the hallway a bit, then came roaring straight at us, I didn't bother to give Gilda any orders.

I just knocked her off her feet.

CHAPTER

"**Y**ou didn't have to do that to me," Gilda said.

"What? You wanted to get hit by a ceramic elephant?"

"You didn't have to push me." She tugged the lapels of her leather jacket. "That's not a nice way to treat a teammate."

"A teammate?"

"Don't talk to me. I'm not talking to you."

We were in the basement of the old church, waiting for the start of our regular nightly meeting.

Cal had six or eight moods he could convey by crossing his arms. This evening, the message I was getting was that he didn't trust himself enough to let his hands get too loose.

"I can't believe it," Cal said to his own knees. "Going after a Tosser in a repo by yourself. Unbelievable."

"But we didn't know the house was repossessed," I protested. "And I wasn't alone. Gilda was with me."

She reared in her metal chair. "I was there, but I wasn't *with* you. How dare you say I was *with* you?"

I looked at Cal. "You get the drift. Another recovering spook was . . . er . . . in the vicinity. Right?"

Cal said, "I'm not talking to you, either."

"Tell me again about the elephant," Fast Eddie said.

Fast Eddie hadn't been interested in my adventure until I got to the part about Dumbo flying between me and Gilda, who had been nudged, ever so gently by a very compassionate friend, out of harm's way. The statue hit the bars with enough force to pop loose a few screws — Why should the house be different from any of us and not have a few loose screws? — and Gilda and I had pushed the bars aside and climbed onto the roof over the porch.

"Any idea where I can get me one of those elephants," Fast Eddie asked. "Maybe I could train it so's it would take me for a ride. Woowee. Wouldn't that be something?"

"I'll keep my eye out for one."

Fast Eddie's glance went from Cal to Gilda, and when his eyeballs rolled back in my direction, an eyebrow arched. "Sorry, son. Didn't mean to be talking to you."

The jury is still out on how much damage a spook could suffer in a repo. Personally, I get no solace from the fact that none of the regulars ever met a specter who took a battering at the hands of a Tosser. If dead men tell no tales, how much conversation should you expect from pulverized dead men?

The precise instant the clock on the wall indicated the start of a new hour, Rosetta announced that Craig was our leader tonight. Craig led, as he always does, with his shame over drowning in his own bed, courtesy of an overflowing waterbed in the apartment on the next floor.

"I'm not sure there's a graceful way of passing on to one's eternal reward. But I would have preferred not to have crossed the Great Divide with a mouthful of water that tasted like cookie crumbs," he said.

Craig, I could tell, had just risen a few notches in Gilda's estimation. Darleen, on the other hand, squirmed and fidgeted and then simply winked herself away. Sometimes she forgets that she doesn't have to be scared about stories about bad things happening to people.

I looked at Cal. He recrossed his arms over his chest in a manner that let me know quite clearly that if I said anything about Craig — especially about whether a spook as rattled as Craig should really know so much about his final hours in the sunshine — we were going to find out exactly how much violence was allowed in the astral plane.

Craig smiled hopefully. "So, I guess that means our topic for this evening is . . . *thanks-a-bunch*."

Everyone groaned.

I raised my hand. I've figured out that Cal couldn't give me a hard time if he's unable to open his mouth. That wouldn't prevent him from button-holing me after the meeting, of course, but for the next sixty minutes I could be content in the knowledge that no one would say they weren't talking to me.

My arm waved in the dusky air like the last reed in the desert. Not another hand stirred, but Craig looked to my left and, as though inviting the wall to bare its soul, said, "Yes?"

"I was looking for some people," a timid female voice whispered. "Actually, a meeting. I think they call themselves a *group*. For folks with . . . ah . . . problems."

I spun around. Margie stood in the soft light of the open door. She wore the same gown as last night, but seemed as fresh as morning dew and greeted me with a sweet, hopeful smile.

"Hello, again," she said.

"Come in, come in," I replied. "Have a seat. Welcome."

Margie settled into the chair next to Gilda that Darleen had vacated a few minutes ago. Gilda's eyes threatened to bulge out of their sockets as she studied the new-arrival without managing to acknowledge her existence.

"This is Margie," I told everyone in the group except Cal. "We met last night while I was checking the streets for newbies. Extending a helping hand to brother — and sister — specters."

Margie's eyes went wide: she could have been looking at me for the first time. "You never really told me about yourself. Does that mean that you're . . . that you're —"

"A carcass. Yes."

Darleen was rematerializing in a chair next to Cal. Upon hearing the dreaded *C* word, she disappeared again in a whimpering *poof*. Fast Eddie lost his fragile hold upon his own concentration and began to sink through the floor. Gilda picked invisible lint from the sleeves of her black jacket.

"Oh, my, there's so much I want to ask you," Margie said. "Does anyone have a pencil? I'm sure I'm going to forget something important."

Roger, who is our resident cynic whenever I decline to defend my title, said, "Nuts, I forgot my pencil, too. And my laptop. And my ability to push an *on* button."

Margie was a picture of bewilderment.

Rosetta jumped in with a smile. "You'll have plenty of opportunity to ask questions after the meeting, dear. This is a time everyone gets to talk, without

CHAPTER

hen the meeting broke up, Margie wore a pained smile. She was dazed and confused as the group's members drifted over to offer words of advice or encouragement. The poor kid was trying to accept that the Pearly Gates and the heavenly choir weren't around the next corner, and she wouldn't be doing brunch any time soon with the Apostles.

Cal snagged me before I could rise from the metal chair. "How's about you showing me that repossessed house. I want to check it out."

"Can we do this later?"

Gilda latched onto Margie as the others left. I started to head their way: It wouldn't do to have our resident Goth stomping on Margie's heart at a moment like this, but Cal blocked my way.

"Has anybody told you that you don't have hormones anymore?" he said. "And you're not allowed to have fantasies."

"I must have slipped out of the orientation class before they got to that."

I tried to maneuver around him. Then I heard the strangest sound which, had my eyes not been fixed on the pair, I would have attributed to the wind. Or the church's old plumbing. Or an auditory hallucination. But my eyes confirmed what my ears were unwilling to believe without someone else backing them up.

Gilda was laughing. I was pretty sure Gilda didn't do laughs.

"*If it's not bringing you further into the spiritual life —*" Cal said, quoting from the program's literature as he managed to follow my eyes without looking up from the floor.

"*— then it's pushing you closer to the sunshine,*" I concluded.

Cal honored me with an approving nod, his gaze finally shifting to Gilda and Margie as they hit the outside stairs. Old habits die hard: Margie was actually putting her feet on the ground. Gilda drifted up the steps like a spook on mission.

"Seriously, kid, something's not right about that one," Cal said.

"Don't let Gilda's looks throw you."

"Naw, I mean the other one."

"Margie? Like what?"

"Like, she's distracting you from recovery."

"What makes you think I'm distracted?" I asked.

"Because you're not asking yourself what's a Tosser doing hanging around a repo? It's too much like dancing with your sister."

"I'll take your word for it, Cal. You know your sister better than me. It's your mother I knew."

Cal growled. I was halfway out the door when he yelled: "Remember, a Tosser's still a specter in need."

Yeah, and a demon is a candidate for spectral anger-management, I said to myself.

By the time I got outside, Margie was gone and Gilda was chatting with Darleen, who must have reappeared to find out if she missed anything important after the discussion of what she usually called *the gooey stuff*. One glance at me, and Darleen said, "Tootle-oo," and dematerialized.

I kept going. Soon I realized Gilda was going, too, only she was right behind me.

When I reached the street, I spun around. She stopped, her interest fixated by a pole at the curb that held a speed limit sign.

I pointed at the grass. "I got here first. You got here second. That means you're following me. And I want you to stop it."

Gilda didn't give me the tiniest fraction of a second to savor my triumph. "That would depend on which way you're going, wouldn't it?" she said.

The kid was trying. I had to remember she'd only been here a night or two. "That was nice of you to talk to Margie after the meeting. The newbies always appreciate a little attention."

"I thought what she said at the meeting was strange." Gilda's eyes flickered over me like the glow of a black flame. "About her last moments. Aren't we supposed to be here a long time before we remember the last moments of our first lives? I can't remember a thing. I don't even know why I'm dressed like this."

Gilda held out her arms for inspection. As Goths go, she wasn't anything special. I've always thought there's no flaw in a woman that couldn't be concealed by a few piercings.

"In the here-after, there aren't any deadlines. To use an unfortunate phrase," I said. "But, yeah, it's odd for someone to drift over the Great Divide with that much information."

"Couldn't that be explained if she'd been here a long, long time? Like Fast Eddie or Rosetta?" Gilda said. If she had veins, I'm sure her blood pressure would have spiked at this point. "I think she's ancient. She's probably been around for centuries. I'll bet she was dead before your great-great-grandmother was even born."

Dead is dead, but the idea of making moon eyes at someone whose earthly remains were now at a molecular level — now, that demands a new standard for commitment. But something else occurred to me.

For a newbie, Gilda had a lot of insight into the working of happily-ever-after.

It had been a while since I'd spent any time on campus. When I was a shaky newbie, Cal and I used to hang around the frat houses on Hamilton Street, making bets on which of the drinkers, which of the drivers and which of the drinking drivers were most likely to show up soonest at the St. Sears group.

I can see now that Cal had been easing my transition into post-life by giving me carefully measured dollops of time in familiar settings. The campus was as good a place as any to look for Fergus. Maybe, like me, he might gravitate during his newbie nights to the places that looked familiar.

"Let's check the campus for angry spirits who throw things," I said.

"Isn't that most of them?"

Like I said, Gilda was so quick on the up-take, if I didn't know better I'd suspect she'd been around the cemetery more than she was admitting.

As we drifted toward the campus, I told her about my early visits there with Cal. How those trips never did trigger any specific memories, but I always left a little sad.

"I never could figure out why the college had that effect on me," I said. "Maybe I was leaving a familiar place. Or maybe it was just being around young people and alcohol. That can be depressing."

"They're missing the best years of their lives," she said. Her eyes had a far-away look. "A total waste. The classes, the gab-fests, the playing footsie, the books."

"Why, Gilda, I didn't know you were such a romantic."

"I only wish I could do it all over," she said. "I wouldn't waste time with that crap. I'd break into a liquor warehouse, and I wouldn't leave until they dragged me here."

"To be young again," I said.

Specters cruising are a sight to behold. Most of us prefer to stay in the middle of the street at tree-level, at least in the brighter communities. It's the only sensible place to be: you can zip down to the sidewalk to take in an instructive quarrel or dart over to a second-floor window if your interests lean to biology.

The thing about cruising in Richmond is that it's an old city. Give a place a little longevity, and its spectral population will only increase. Give it a touch of nostalgia, and the spooks start coming out of the woodwork. Literally.

The sky above Monument Avenue was so dense with night-time traffic, you could practically walk from the upper branches of trees on the northern side to their counterparts on the southern by stepping on the shoulders of gawkers from the astral plane.

Farmers from an age when bib-overalls weren't a fashion statement, country gentlemen from a time before *bedroom communities*, soldiers from an era when *a smart weapon* was an infantryman who could read — all moved in orderly corridors above the roadway.

Especially the soldiers. Every rube who once wore a gray uniform and thought the phrase *Rest in Peace* didn't apply to him, was here. Some traveled, parade-ground fashion, in neat rows and columns; others drifted in small groups or alone. Yokels in uniform who were wide-eyed and slack-jawed with the big city, a hundred and fifty years after the war.

"You're wasting your time here, you know," Gilda said.

"Hmmm?"

"Your little Margie. The chick isn't a newbie."

I hadn't mentioned Margie. I didn't intend to mention Margie. The more I thought about her the less inclined I was to say a word.

"Fergus. We're here to find Fergus."

"Right."

An astral tour passed down the street. We paused a moment to wave back at the group.

"I could tell by her hands," Gilda continued.

"You seem to know a lot about the afterlife. For someone who just got here."

"I just pay attention, is all."

"Then pay attention to this, "I snapped. "How old a spook looks isn't tied to his age at check-out."

"Some of us can tell these things," Gilda mumbled.

Overhead, an ancient rebel collided with a smartly dressed fellow in a smoking-jacket and spats. The reb staggered, reached to retrieve his hat, was buffeted again by a couple of young specters on astral skateboards and ended up doing a half-gainer toward the ground.

The soldier was terrified as he fell. I've never seen anyone come apart so quickly. I mean, go to pieces in such a hurry. Or to be more precise: most of his left leg tumbled out of his trousers and fell toward the far side of the street, his right arm accelerated into a mansion on the other side, a few ribs popped from his blouse and zeroed in on some breathers strolling on the sidewalk, and his right thigh bone arced toward the lawn where Gilda and I stood.

"You don't see that every day," I said.

"I heard last night some old witch's nasty bits fell through the roof of a Baptist Church. I guess, so long as she wasn't dancing or drinking when it happened, it'll be okay."

"No, I mean *that*." I pointed to the grass between sidewalk and curb where the rebel's leg bone lay. "Usually, they hit the ground and keep going."

Gilda winced. "You're right." She bent over, and I half-expected her to try engaging the former leg in a conversation. "It doesn't look like it's sinking."

"I guess it's been fighting to stay on this side of the roots for so long, it'll just continue doing that from force of habit."

"Do you think the old-timer will come back for it?"

"I think the old boy is riding the wind."

Riding the wind – gone to the everlasting *poof*, snuck off for a smoke and lost his way back to the meeting, grew bored with the eternal questions and resigned from specterhood.

Gilda moved on. Something in the shadows caught my eye. Something reminiscent of Margie, although it couldn't possibly be her. Why should Margie be crawling on the ground around a tree?

As the creature crept from the darkness, its features resolved into a familiar form. A dog. A long-eared, short-legged canine with eyes of such liquidity and feeling that, for a moment, I convinced myself it was on the verge of asking me a question.

"A beagle!" Gilda squealed. She squatted beside the dog's black-white-and-brown coat. If I hadn't known better, I could have imagined the dog was watching Gilda's hand.

Even doubters of the paranormal concede that animals can be aware of things beyond the normal sensory range. Cal says they don't really see us. They have a rough idea that something is happening outside the ordinary, and they have a general sense of where, whatever it is, is.

This beagle was immobile while Gilda was beside her, and when Gilda arose, the dog slowly ambled toward the bone.

"Aw, isn't that cute," Gilda said.

There's something about a woman with purple fingernails and the wardrobe of a Goth warrior saying *That's cute* that's more amazing than the spontaneous disassembly of a Civil War veteran. I wondered if I was being foolish for not following Darleen's example and treating my afterlife's unpleasant moments with a *poof*.

Leaning over the spectral bone, the beagle whined and pawed where the femur was supposed to be, even opened its mouth delicately and tried to snag the bone.

I had trouble accepting what was going on. I don't mean the slow cavalcade of three centuries' decedents twenty feet above a city street or the fact of my own partial existence in a world that gave me my exit papers some time ago. I was having trouble accepting that the dog was actually seeing a spook's bone.

"Oh, this is silly," I said.

I picked up the bone. The dog's eyes appeared to follow the bone as I waved it in the air. The beagle's gaze tracked the movements of both my arm and the vet's leg, neither one of which the animal was supposed to be able to see.

"Give it to me," Gilda asked.

Once I handed it over, she checked the procession overhead and, detecting an opening in the crowd, pitched the bone into the darkness. I saw it slice through the trees on the other side of the street, but whether it fell to the ground or sank into the earth or was retrieved by an old soldier who was in need of body parts, I cannot say.

I was unhappy, though, to see the dog run away.

Seven
CHAPTER

al says we're spending the here-after in Richmond because it's a place we never lived, but to which we have some emotional connection. Whether that's wisdom inscribed on a tablet someplace or an example of Cal winging it is anybody's guess. I've got to admit it makes sense whenever I see the hordes of Rebel soldiers who died on distant battlefields but ended up, spectrally, in central Virginia because it was the capital of their short-lived nation.

As far as I can tell, Richmond had no connection with my days in the sunshine. There have been no *deja vu* moments on the nights I've wandered across downtown or into the suburbs. No memories of entering a particular movie theater, school or restaurant during my late, ambulatory period.

This little inside-the-hearse nugget is necessary to understand what happened after Gilda and I had spent a couple more hours drifting around the frat houses on Hamilton. The longer we wandered, the less I understood what I was doing there. So, when Gilda suggested we check out Cary Street for signs of Fergus, I agreed, barely noticing that it might be more likely for someone like Margie to be there.

Cary Street is where Richmond goes to be trendy. Any place that has the state's highest concentration per city block of antique stores and ice cream parlors can't be ignored.

Lights were brighter here than on Monument or Hamilton, which required the ghostly traffic to shift ten or fifteen feet higher above the street. The odd rebel soldier joined the cavalcade; yet, most of the passers-by on the astral plane were small-town folks and farmers from the late 1800s or early 1900s who died perhaps regretting they never visited the big city.

We stayed at ground level in the shadows of the side streets. Since the light was artificial, we could go onto the main drag if we wanted, although it wasn't very comfortable. Have you ever wanted to scratch the underside of your fingernails or the interior of a tooth? If you have, you'll know what I'm talking about.

I watched a half-dozen female spooks dressed up for *Little House on the Prairie* swoop down to cluster around one of the breathers on the sidewalk like a flock of over-sized pigeons, clucking and cooing, and then darting up again into the darkness.

"How can they do that?" Gilda muttered. "Get so close to those weird creatures?"

"The breathers don't know we're here. They can't see us."

"I'm not talking about the breathers."

I studied my companion. She must have a monopoly on the here-after's supply of eyeliner, purple nail polish, silver chains and black fabric. Her eyes followed a couple co-eds in blonde pony-tails, jeans that had been ironed and starched, and form-fitting blouses. They were window-shopping, and when they turned away from a display of formal gowns, laughing and talking, I saw a shudder pass from the tips of Gilda's scuffed black boots to the top of her spiked hair.

"Horrible, horrible," she whispered.

I moved off the sidewalk to keep a middle-aged jogger from running through me. Gilda gave him a sneer, as though daring him to ruffle a transcendent entity such as herself. The jogger swerved around her.

"You're comfortable being dead, aren't you?" I said. "I mean, you didn't give up much when you came here."

"Cigarettes, booze and sex."

"Well, yeah, there's that. But besides that?"

Gilda kicked a fallen leaf that didn't know her foot was there. Head down, she crossed the street to an alley paralleling Cary. "I think I spent my entire life trying to get here."

I waited for an SUV driven by a little old lady to pass before going into the street. Gilda didn't miss a beat as the machine swept through her, and I caught myself wondering if Gilda's indifference was a mark of someone who had truly accepted her current condition. Perhaps I was still squeamish about walking through people and vehicles because I didn't want to get into the habit. Because, deep down, I expected someday to return to the sunlight.

That might mean I should be sitting at Gilda's booted feet to learn the great truths that had eluded me.

Gilda marched toward a cat sitting on the lid of a garbage can. The animal's back was arched, its tail raised, the hair on its body stood straight up. It knew something was there in the night, an unknown thing, which might be a danger, and which was moving toward her.

The cat was on the tippy-toes of its pads, Gilda a couple feet away. Then this newbie to our group, who seemed to have this intuitive grasp of the mysteries of eternity, jumped into the night air, her arms and legs working like windmills, shouting, "BOO!"

I've been wrong about spooks before.

We spent the rest of the night along Cary, sometimes hanging out with members of our 12-step group, sometimes drifting alone, taking in the sights, talking about the program, gossiping (which we're strictly forbidden to do, but, hey, we're only spectral) about the St. Sears members who look like they may be sneaking out in the mornings to take a nip of sunshine.

I saw Hank down the block, checking out a motorcycle that was as big as a mid-sized car, and waved for him to come join us. Hank waved and turned back to the motorcycle.

"He doesn't like me," Gilda muttered.

"That's not true," I said. Still, I decided it'd be better not to get in the middle of any discussion involving both Hank and Gilda.

At some point, a dog decided to tag along. I can't say I've spent much time with a dog trotting along beside me, but I'd come to accept that our presence intrigues some creatures, especially the domesticated variety.

Gilda said this was the same beagle we'd met earlier, the one who'd tried to retrieve the old rebel's leg bone.

I squatted to look the animal in the eye. The beagle cocked her head to one side and studied me. Or, I should say, seemed to study me. For these critters only have the haziest perceptions of us. This dog, however, hadn't been informed of her own limitations: she fixed her large, warm eyes directly on mine, and when I stretched out a hand toward the top of her head – knowing full well that my fingers could sink to the center of her skull without any trouble – the dog closed her eyes and lolled her head to one side. I could have sworn she was preparing to be stroked.

"She likes you," Gilda said.

"She doesn't know I'm here. It's just a coincidence."

"Right."

Sometime after midnight, we caught up with Fast Eddie and Rosetta – talk about improbable couples – and went to a little restaurant off Beauregard where the lights were low enough not to be bothersome. We found a booth free of breathers where we could act as though we were a typical four-some waiting two hours for service in a dive that was nearly empty.

The last occupants had left on the table a ring of water from a drinking glass. I tried to squeegee it away with, of course, no success. But that didn't stop me from trying.

"Did you ever wonder," I said, "if coming to places like this is bad for us? *If you're not getting better at being dead, you're slipping deeper into fantasies of resurrection.*"

Everyone knew the line from our literature, but none of the others were bothered by play-acting from time to time that we were normal . . . let's say the *P* word . . . people.

Rosetta crinkled her nose. "Then where should we go and what should we do? Lie under the ground in our coffins?"

A thought struck me like a lightning bolt. "Maybe that's why we don't know what we're doing here. Maybe jumping back into our caskets and being very, very quiet is what we're supposed to be doing all along."

Rosetta went, "Ooow."

Gilda glared at the table, as though suspecting it of harboring plans for sudden, aggressive moves.

Fast Eddie cackled, and a goldfish leaped in its little bowl by the cash register. A fellow three tables over, who was working his way through a pot of coffee, getting himself sober enough to return home, straightened as though ice cubes had been dumped down the back of his shirt. And a tray of silverware slid from the hands of a passing waitress and crashed on the floor.

"They're playing with us, son," Fast Eddie told me. "Just making a game of it."

"Who is?" I asked.

"Whoever's in charge."

"You mean the Uber-spirit?" Rosetta whispered.

"I mean the big cheese, the boss man, the ultimate kahuna. The guy who makes up the rules and keeps the keys."

"*A man*," Gilda said; it was clearly the ugliest word she could think of.

On that cheerful note, we decided to call it a night. Fast Eddie and Rosetta dematerialized in the booth. Gilda sat with her hands in her lap and her head down; her eyes, however, darted all over the place, and I half-wondered if she was trying to make out some music I couldn't hear.

But what I actually thought she was hearing was the thunderous sound of nothing coming from me. No invitations to come back to my shack on the island, no plans for getting together tomorrow, nothing involving her. After all, I hadn't come this far in the ever-after to spend all my time with a Goth.

She caught my eye, said, "Later," and left with a *poof.*

Talk about the Uber-spirit in my 12-step group always makes me uncomfortable. I'd never been what anyone would call a believer, and part of me thought I'd be a real hypocrite to get religious now. It's not as though I'd stumbled into streets of gold or found myself chatting about the weather with an archangel.

I guess what I'm saying is that, if there is an Uber-spirit, I hope to get points for consistency by staying true to my non-beliefs to the end. And beyond.

Passing through the restaurant's door, I found the beagle stretched on her belly on the sidewalk. She scrambled to her feet and looked at me with adoration. Okay, I was coming to admit the animal might actually see me, and she appreciated that I'd been willing to play with her by wiggling a bone for her to fetch. We can overlook the fact the original owner might want it back.

I squatted. "If I was a breather, I'd march into that restaurant and order you their biggest, juiciest steak. I want you to know that."

The beagle was excited. She must have heard the word *steak* and was hoping that I'd come through.

"You just hang on a little more, okay? Somebody will get you that steak. I know they will. Just hang on."

Playful, angry and vengeful are the three approved emotions for spooks that I remember from my sunshine days. Let me tell you, we can cover the waterfront, emotion-wise, and at that moment, as I straightened and left the dog, I was feeling so low I could have thrown myself into the Atlantic and sunk lower than whale poop.

Hang on. I'll have it emblazoned on my personal coat of arms once I get around to ordering a set. Hang on, because that's what I do, that's what I've always done, and I don't know another way of putting the nights together.

Any doubts whether the dog could actually see me were dispelled when I looked down and saw the beagle running below me on the sidewalk. I glided back to the ground.

Eight

CHAPTER

I didn't have any idea about how far we were from my bucket on Belle Island, nor how long it would take to get there at a breather's pace. Still, dawn had to be a couple hours away, so I let the beagle lead me through the alleys along Cary.

At the back door of several restaurants, we found enough dropped, dribbled or spilled food to keep up the dog's strength. One place actually set a tray on top of a garbage can with sandwiches, bottles of water and bite-sized pieces of fresh fruit and vegetables.

Three street-people loitered on the ground, with their backs to the restaurant's wall and their food on white paper napkins on their laps.

"No, girl," I whispered. "Let's go this way. We don't know those people."

But the dog scampered to the little group. Truth be told, I wasn't worried about someone abusing the animal. I was afraid the dog would realize that real people could get her food and I couldn't.

A vagrant shooed the dog away. The second offered her a taste of his sandwich. The third, a young woman with short blonde hair and socks knitted with the colors of the rainbow, went to the tray and returned with sandwich meat, a generous slice of chicken breast and the bone from a T-bone steak.

The feast had barely hit the ground before the beagle devoured the sandwich meat and the chicken. Then, after snatching the bone, she waddled confidently toward me. She stretched on her stomach and, holding the bone in place with her front paws, proceeded to chomp away every remnant of meat, then gnawed the bone for whatever was left.

Such unashamed joy from food made me wonder if I'd ever found such pleasure in what I ate. Or ever had real respect for the sensation of taste.

Raised voices drew my attention to the end of the alley. I looked up and, for an instant, believed I'd truly died and gone to heaven. There amid the trash cans, litter and graffiti was an angel. Clothed in a white gown that glowed in the darkness, her chin tilted engagingly as she looked with a small, calm smile at a breather barely three feet away.

"I didn't know the beautiful spooks came here," I called out.

Margie turned to me and — these moments happen every night, but they're still a little unnerving — the breather stopped talking and glanced in my direction, too. Maybe the breather sensed something or maybe she heard a noise from the dog or one of the street-people that eluded me.

Margie seemed to speak to her and, in another of those coincidences that are part of death, the woman turned around and walked away.

"You've got to stop that," I said.

"Stop what?"

"Talking to breathers."

"But I am a breather," she said. Margie got fluttery, and I realized what set her apart from the spooks I spent my here-after with — besides having the toughest sense of denial that I'd ever heard of. She actually cared what others thought about her. I guess that's another big *plus* that I've gotten these nights. Once you've been tossed into a casket, peoples' opinions of you start to lose their sting.

"You really shouldn't have disappeared after the meeting this evening," I said. "If you hang around with the gang, you'll learn the ropes a lot faster."

"Well, I'm hanging around you, aren't I?"

If somebody on this side of the curtain fires up your hormones, get to me immediately, I remember Cal telling me. *Don't worry about a graceful exit. Worry about what I'll do to your sorry little ectoplasmic butt when I get my hands on you.*

When Cal shared those pearls of wisdom with me, I was stunned to learn some old feelings might step into the batter's box again. And, now that I was actually in that situation, all I could think about was how far this stuff went. Did

Casper the Friendly Ghost and little Wendy try posthumous hanky-panky inside their old mansion?

"Yes, you certainly are hanging around with me." I scuffed a toe in the dirt, but only succeeded in burying my foot in the ground.

"Can you tell me something?" she asked.

"Sure." I couldn't stop grinning.

"These *breathers* — I think that's what you called them — how can you tell them apart from people like you and me?"

"Mainly, it's that they're in the physical world. They cast shadows, see themselves in mirrors, can touch objects and each other. And they'll pass through us like a cold wind through an attic."

"But I can touch you."

"My point exactly," I said.

"Where do you live?" A cloud of pink puffed into her cheeks. "I mean, where are you when you're not wandering around?"

"I hang my bucket down by the river."

"Hang your bucket?"

Boy, did Margie have a lot to learn, but before I could reply, a low whimpering caught my attention. The beagle had decided to join us, bringing, of course, its bone.

"Oh, what a cute puppy!" Margie squatted down and extended her hands toward the dog.

"Don't!" I shouted, then, more softly added: "You'd better not do that."

"She's not going to bite me."

"I'm concerned with what you'll do to her." I held my hand a few inches above the dog's head, which seemed to calm her. "If you try to touch her, what's going to happen?"

"You think she'll bite me?"

"No, I'm talking about your hand," I said, continuing as Margie looked at me with an expression remarkably like the beagle's. "Your hand will pass through the animal's body. You won't kill her, probably won't even hurt her. But the dog will know that your hand is somewhere inside her and she'll freak out. Probably just the way you feel when you pass through someone on the street."

Deer in the headlights would look pepped up and hyper-vigilant next to the other-worldly stare I got from Margie.

"You mean," I said, "you haven't had someone walk right through you? Never had a car pass through your body?"

"Hmmm?"

My doubts about lingering hormones disappeared at that moment. I've always been a sucker for a damsel in distress. And a specter in distress is even more . . . well . . . haunting.

"Why don't you join my little furry friend and me? We're taking in the night air. What do you say?"

I reached for her arm. She bounded halfway into the street.

"Look," she said, "I don't want to seem unappreciative. But I'm new here. I don't really know my way around. And we barely know each other. There's no rush, is there? I mean, after all, we have all the time in the world."

"Technically, we've already used all our time in one world. The clock's running on us now in the after-world."

"Oh, that's so cute. Funniest thing I've heard . . . here . . . wherever it is. You've got a way with words, Mister." All said while backing across the street and up a driveway to the other sidewalk.

"Ralph, my name is Ralph." I called. "And don't forget the meeting tomorrow night."

"I wouldn't miss it for the world. I mean, this world. But the other world, too. I wouldn't miss it for all the worlds in . . . the . . . world."

Yeah, I know. Some guys have that effect on women.

The beagle and I followed the back-alley along Cary for a couple more blocks. None of the restaurants were so scrupulous in their garbage disposal that the pup's well-tuned nose couldn't find a morsel or two.

We crossed the main drag and headed for the river, and I realized my companion was getting droopy. A few times, passing trees, she made the obligatory search around the trunk and, once out of my sight, lay down. Each time, she staggered to her feet and hustled after me when I started gliding away.

As I said, I can't remember when I last traveled any great distance in real-time. *Stop and smell the roses* doesn't carry any weight with someone who once shared a hearse with a hundred pounds of gardenias.

Which is why I started to worry when I could actually see the delineation between the sky and the eastern horizon. I bent over to carry the beagle and my arms went clear through the creature.

The dog yelped, jumped back, and gave me a look that said, in any language from any species in any plane of existence: *What's wrong with you, Sucker?* But, at least, the dog picked up the pace.

Belle Island is connected to the mainland by a concrete walkway. Perhaps if I were a better spook, I would have realized something was wrong that night when I made out the outlines of the shack that I call home. Even a mediocre psychic would have sensed disturbances in the cosmic order before I stumbled over the rock garden in front of the shack.

The rock garden?

I eased to one side to take advantage of the gray light seeping over the eastern rim of the world. Before me on the ground, which was supposed to be as bare and hard as seasoned concrete, was a jumble of stones, bricks, rocks and pebbles. Nothing larger than a softball, but in sheer volume representing three or four wheelbarrows of stuff.

The beagle whined. I appreciated the sympathy.

When I left this evening, the shack could have appeared in any dictionary next to the word *ramshackle*. Now it was an illustration for *war-torn*. The tin roof had been battered, popped and buckled by a deluge of stones, large sections punctured by falling debris of various sizes, and the walls had been beaten by a rain of missiles that perforated most of the weathered planks and splintered the rest.

If the shack hadn't been erected in a city that regarded stubbornness as a civic virtue, it would have collapsed into a pile of kindling.

"That old shack sure must have irritated somebody."

Gilda had materialized beside me. Her black leather jacket, black skirt and black tights merged with the shadows, making her little more than a glowing face and fidgety white fingers.

"What are you doing here?" I asked.

"Well, I got to thinking about what we talked about. Especially what we didn't talk about."

"*Didn't talk about?* That covers a lot of territory."

Gilda winced. "I mean, what I didn't talk about."

I was perfectly willing to wave away the subject, offer to have a nice long chat tomorrow night and hope Gilda forgot this conversation by then. I wanted to get only so close to a specter who wore chains.

But Specters Anonymous says I'm supposed to help *the poor, still-suffering spook*. What's comfortable for me doesn't enter into it.

"What's that?" I hoped I didn't sound as helpless as I felt.

"I'm not a newbie." Her chest heaved. "I was in this other group. In Portland."

"Portland, Maine, or Portland, Oregon?"

"Yes."

The steel was back in her eyes until I said, "I see."

"One of them took me aside after a meeting a few nights ago. He said I'd fit in better someplace else. He said I was —"

"You were —?"

"Too dark."

I didn't know what worried me more — having Fergus find a clump of astral Kryptonite that'd knock me out of this plane of existence, or letting Gilda see the slightest twitch of muscles that might indicate the formation of a smirk.

"There's no accounting for some spooks," I said.

Gilda took the news stoically, then, not one to dally over her own feelings, said, "I don't think your bucket in there is going to be a safe place to bed down for the day."

Nodding, I scanned the buildings along the shore. Several were abandoned factories or warehouses, where a homeless spook might expect to find a quiet, dark corner to spend the next twelve hours or so. Still, that's not the kind of decision to make on the fly.

"It'll work out," I said, adding to the dog, "Maybe you know someplace you'd recommend."

The dog, who stretched out on the ground again, arched her ears when I spoke to her. Ever hopeful the conversation would eventually involve ground beef.

"You put me up last morning," Gilda said. "I can return the favor and offer you a place today."

A faint suggestion of pink stained the distant skyline. I was running out of time. And a spook caught for long in the open in the sunlight wouldn't have to worry about the likes of Fergus.

"I think we'd better do that," I answered. "Thanks."

Then, turning to the dog, I said, "Ready to get some shut-eye, girl? Then come on. Let's get a move on. Night's a-wasting."

The dog pulled herself up from the ground, but Gilda hunched down beside her and said, "I don't think she can come with us. We don't have time."

"There's plenty of time," I protested, but glancing toward the east saw a blood-red smear at the base of the sky. "Well, maybe not."

I went to the dog and, squatting down, held my hand over the animal's head. The beagle, sensing she was about to be coddled and petted, lay down again.

"You'll be fine, girl. You're a good dog, a very good dog."

And as the pink traces of day touched the quiet air and the dog fell quickly into a deep sleep, Gilda and I slipped away.

CHAPTER

pecters Anonymous traces its beginning to what the old-timers call *our fumbling around period*. Specters were beginning to clear their thoughts from the roller-coaster ride of living, and a few pioneers realized that only by banding together and *sharing our perplexities, tremors and fantasies* (another line from the official text) could we hope to recover from our obsession with having beating hearts.

We had to accept the fact that we were powerless over life, that without the support and wisdom of those who had *kicked the sunshine habit* we were going to continue to trick ourselves into thinking we could be breathers again.

Central to our transcendence is the need to have a fixed place to bed down each morning. It's not as important as going to meetings or having a sponsor, but hey, the odds of avoiding a stumblie start leaning in your favor if you're tucked away someplace safe and dark when the early bird starts looking for its breakfast.

Unspoken in questions of lodging is the idea of avoiding breathers. Partly for the same reason that halfway houses generally aren't located above bars. Partly because the pre-deceased have a tendency to open curtains, pull up blinds, leave outside doors open and act as though they own the world.

So, I was surprised when Gilda took me — via the usual *Beam-me-up-Scotty* route — to the new townhouses south of Shockoe Bottom along the river.

I scanned the windows facing the water: all had curtains.

"You're kidding, right?" I asked. "Or is one of these places vacant?"

Gilda had a sheepish grin. "Trust me on this one. You're going to love it."

Dawn had definitely arrived, and red light was reflecting from the windows. The air hummed with a couple thousand insects preparing themselves for another day to eat or be eaten.

"*Trust me.* Isn't that what the spider said to the fly?"

"Yep. And the funeral director to his newest customer."

Gilda glided through the front door of a townhouse and, seeing plenty of sunlight approaching from the east and no good avenues for retreat, I followed.

I guess you could call the place nice if you weren't bothered by thick wall-to-wall carpets of a hard-to-define shade of orange, furniture of the upscale variety that one collected instead of merely bought, and an overall shortage of cobwebs.

A small airplane lay on a coffee table, a model jet fighter that someone was gluing together.

"You're bringing me to a place with kids?"

Gilda nodded, obviously feeling smug.

"How many? What ages?"

"One. And nine-ish."

"Those are two very bad numbers."

She shrugged. When a dead Goth shows signs of indifference, it's time to move on to another subject.

"Why here?" I asked.

"Let me show you," Gilda added and drifted into the next room.

Just below the ceiling of the dining room on two walls were narrow shelves holding coffee pots. Dozens of coffee pots. A few must have been antiques, many were just odd. They were made of brass, glass, ceramics and aluminum. Plug-in percolators, stove-top percolators, campfire percolators. There were animal shapes, animal paintings, flower paintings, pastoral scenes, hunting scenes, stamped seascapes, round spouts, square spouts, triangular spouts and spouts that looped back over themselves like knots.

Gilda said, "It's heaven. Nobody's going to take one of those pots down. And you wake up surrounded by the smell of coffee. It's to-die-for."

"That rules us out."

Why wasn't I surprised that Gilda wasn't listening? With a dreamy smile, she drifted into the spout of a pot decorated with inlaid pictures of coffee beans.

I heard a creak on the steps to the second floor and zipped through the stubby spout of a battered pot that must have belonged to a hobo. Who didn't use the pot only for coffee.

Aside from a slight soapy scent and the smell of a wet dog, I passed an uneventful day in my new bucket.

I'll say this for being dead: It gives you a real appreciation for waking up. I pop up after my daily snooze with more vim and vigor than I had when a little enthusiasm might have done me good.

I heard the unmistakable sound of a rock rolling down a steep roof, and I darted out of the pot to catch the Tosser in the act. (What I was going to do once I got him was, for the moment, a technicality.)

The dining room lay in shadows; a table lamp in the living room cast an off-white glow that let me see a softball roll on the hardwood floor in the foyer to the living room's thick carpet. Moments later came the same, singular, Tosser-at-work sound:

Wwwwwwrrrrr-THUMP, wwwwwrrrrr-THUMP, wwwwwrrrrr-THUMP.

I peered around a corner in time to see another softball roll to the edge of a bare step, drop to the next step, then proceed along. Like ectoplasm rolling down a Ferris wheel after a disaster at the state fair. You'll understand what I'm saying later.

The arrival of the second softball on the ground-floor was accompanied by a maternal voice from the other side of the dining room:

"James William, are you rolling your father's softballs on the stairs?"

"No, ma'am."

I hadn't seen the kid, and already I liked him.

When he appeared, James William came with small fingers covered by traces of at least seven different kinds of food and three major categories of grime. His hair was brown and plastered across his forehead, and he had freckles lining the bridge of his nose.

Gilda appeared at my side. "Have you figured out why I brought you here?"

"To show off the love-child you had with Fast Eddie?"

"Just because I'm dead, doesn't mean I'm tasteless."

The edges of her eyeliner wrinkled, and I suspected that if Gilda weren't very, very careful, she was going to be caught actually committing a smile.

"Besides showing me your legendary skills as a babysitter, what else made you bring me here?" I asked.

In fact, the kid's screams had pinned my spectral ears to the sides of my head and deadened my hearing. Who could have guessed one of the hazards of entering the Great Silence was deafness? I mean, what is the point?

I felt a headache coming on. Dare I call it the ghost of a headache?

Gilda, on the other hand, seemed rather pleased with James William, my discomfort and, most especially, herself.

Drifting down again to get a good look at the DVD, wondering if I could squeeze myself onto the disc and see the shows by running around the DVD very fast, I said to her:

"You wouldn't happen to be one of those paranormal specters?"

"*Normal* specters," she corrected. "We're already in the paranormal. So the powers that breathers consider paranormal would be normal for us."

"Let me try again." I was definitely getting a headache. "So, you are a normal specter?"

"No, I'm paranormal. Can't levitate a thimble, frighten a new-born kitten or possess a fly."

"You threw a rock at my shack."

Gilda glanced at her fingers. "I'm not doing that again. I broke a nail."

"Just for the record"– Sighing, I leered at the glittery disc –"would you be able to lift a DVD, carry it about eight inches, drop it into a tray and punch a power button?"

"*And* punch the button? You want all that, plus punching a button?"

"Yes."

Gilda chewed on her lower lip. "Nah. Can't do any of it."

"That's it. That's the absolute limit. I've had enough. Transcendence or no transcendence, program or no program, I am now going to become a wailing banshee."

"Banshees are chicks, man. You can't become a banshee." Gilda eyed me suspiciously. "Not unless there's something intimately personal that you haven't told me."

"There is nothing *intimately personal* that I ever told you, ever intended to tell you, or ever could be induced, cajoled, badgered or threatened into telling you."

"Nothing you want to share with a teammate?" she said.

"Team?" I asked. "What team? What makes you think we're a team?"

If Gilda had been a Tosser, I knew that at that moment I would have been buried under the living room furniture, the upstairs furniture, the walls and ceiling, plus the neighbor's townhouse and the six closest oaks on the street.

But I had something else on my mind. I could see right through Gilda, in a practical sense, and my attention was caught by a waving little shadow, right next to James William, who had returned to the living room and was looking down with an expression of sheer wonder.

Leaning to one side, I tried to get a clear view behind Gilda of what James William was looking at. Gilda went *poof* with a squinty glare and an attitude that would take a recovering specter four meetings and two long talks with his sponsor to explain.

On the plus side, Gilda was no longer blocking my view. I was able to tie together into a neat, wiggling, foul-breathed bundle of fur both the strange waving shadow I'd noticed and James William's grin.

The beagle was back.

CHAPTER Ten

'll give the dog credit. Although the animal seemed to realize James Williams had the edge over me when it came to scratching its neck and dishing up the occasional hamburger, I really believe the beagle respected me for having tried to provide a little *boeuf du Rebel*.

The idea of a dog walking around Richmond with a ghost's leg in its chops gave me an idea. I squatted, put on my most appealing, canine-friendly smile and patted my hands. "Come here, girl. Come on over and say howdy to your old pal Ralph."

You'd think the poor animal had gone a month without any attention. She scampered across the rug, her tongue lashing wildly and her eyes beaming, and when she reached me, she thrust her nose into my out-stretched hands. Or, being sensitive to different planes of existence, she thrust her nose into the empty air where my hands were spectrally stretched.

I steeled myself from the urge to play with the beagle; there was, after all, a job to be done. So I let the dog have a clear view of the TV table. I patted the DVD.

"You can do it. Yes, you can. Just pick up the nice little disc. Give it a try. Come on."

One step at a time, that was the game-plan. I'd worry later how to persuade the dog to drop the disc into the player's tray and push the start button.

James William had other ideas. "You want to watch TV, girl? Here, let me help you."

The kid rushed up, the dog and I scrambled out of his way, and soon I heard the tantalizing click and whine of a DVD player going about its business. I had planned all along for that to happen. Sure, I had.

I sat down next to the beagle, my hand rubbing the air inches from her shoulders. For her part, the dog was quite the diplomat: she pretended our almost-petting session was a terrific back rub.

The screen sputtered and flickered. Ghostly music rose from the speakers, something so familiar, yet terrifying. A shiver ran down my ectoplasmic spine. The music kept playing, voices joined in with lyrics, and I got a sick feeling. Suddenly, the screen was purple and smiling in a faintly prehistoric way.

James Williams lowered his nose until it brushed the dog's snout. "Do you like Barney, too? Huh? What do you say?"

The beagle looked at the boy, then me. A kind of awkward despair filled her large brown eyes.

"Keep the kid happy," I whispered. "I'll be okay. Really."

Footsteps sounded on the wooden floor of the hallway, the pace steady, hitting the boards with the impact of twin sixteen-pound hammers. The beagle jumped to her feet and darted to the archway to the hall.

Looking down the hallway, the animal froze. The footsteps stopped. The air vibrated with muted uncertainty.

A woman's voice ripped the silence. "Who let that animal into my house? James William!"

Sooner or later, every newbie who materializes in Richmond finds his spectral feet gliding the herringbone-patterned bricks at Madame Sophie's. Some weekend nights the traffic above Soph's street rivals Monument Avenue. Tonight, the sidewalk outside her establishment was relatively quiet: either Soph had decided to give specterhood a break by getting into her apricot brandy early or the Hindus were planning a mass reincarnation at their ashram in the suburbs.

I like Soph. There's a certain charm in the neon sign in her bay-window — *Psychic Adviser* — and the way a crack in the glass seems to place a question mark between the two words. The interior smelled of mold and rain-rotted timbers. The curtains and furniture coverings were of fabrics reserved these days for carpets. And the newest thing in the place was the crystal ball that lay on a black velvet cloth.

Soph is a woman of indeterminate age. Somewhere between 104 and 115 is my guess. Or that may just be the age of the powder that's caked so heavily on her face that Hank swears he once saw a baby mouse peek out from a crease between her nose and lip.

Soph's appeal to both the specter-set and breathers is that she actually has some ability. Think of an old radio with a dial to tune it to stations. Try to remember what it was like, slowly working that dial late at night, when the slightest twitch of the dial brought in voices and snatches of music that had the half-life of a single flap of a firefly's wing. That's the extent of Soph's contact with the spirit world.

On a good night, when the wind was from the west and Soph hadn't spent too much time with her *medicine*, she could pick up the odd phrase or two that newbies were trying to get to folks from their first lives.

Of course, for those of us who believe recovery for a spook entails accepting that the world of breathers has nothing to do with us, Madame Sophie, in her own sweet-hearted, semi-competent, boozy way, can keep a lot of specters from moving on.

Before I entered the front door, I could hear the chaos inside.

"Speak to me, Gilbert, speak." That's Soph. "I command you to part the curtains of darkness and let your voice be heard."

"If you'd shut up, you old hag, I'd be able to get in a word from time to time." That must be Gilbert.

"Be not afraid, Gilbert. This is a universe of love. We are all your friends."

"Yes, Gilbert. Talk to me. A hundred times each day, I think I can almost hear your voice." That must be wifey, mom or sis. "Especially, when I'm alone in that great big bed of ours."

Let's rule out mom and sis for now.

"Gilbert, I command you to talk to this woman."

"I'm trying. I'm trying."

When I made it to the parlor, it was pretty easy to tell the newbies from the spooks who've spent a few nights in specterdom. The new-arrivals were arranged in the couches and chairs lining the walls, although, being newbies, they spent most of the time floating through cushions or into the ceiling. The old-timers were crowded into the little room off the parlor.

Rosetta, from my group, was there. "Gilbert," she said. "This is not the way. Oh, what's that phrase the newbies use? —You're toast."

"*Accept not the toast*," Sophie intoned. "*Drink not the proffered libation.* Gilbert feels most strongly about this."

"I do not, you old witch."

"Who are you calling a witch?" Rosetta bristled.

"That doesn't sound like my Gilbert," wifey pouted.

"But I see him most clearly." Sophie moves fast when the client gets restless. "He is dressed in a garment that blazes like the sun. His skin has a magical luster. He is surrounded by a host of the heavenly choir."

"Garments? Luster? Heavenly choir? What are you, some kind of nut?" This, of course, from Gilbert.

Wifey claps her hands. Sophie has a sly smile. Rosetta is convinced that Gilbert will understand her if she gets under his nose. Gilbert is convinced the problem is that he's not talking loudly and slowly enough.

I'm convinced Fergus would rather camp out under a heating lamp than come here.

So, I *poofed* into the basement room of the St. Sears group. The breathers who had their own 12-step meeting a couple hours before must have just wrapped it up. They left the room with the comforting scent of coffee, which gave the newbies an incentive not to drift through the seats of the gray metal chairs.

Fast Eddie looked up. Something clattered to the floor. I saw a coffee bean roll under a chair.

"You old scoundrel," I said. "You were levitating it."

"The wind must have knocked it off a chair."

"There's no wind in here. Besides, what's a coffee bean doing on a chair?"

I've always been partial to Fast Eddie. He has an edge. I watched the old reprobate make quick calculations about how he was going to talk his way out of this one, ideally with a spin or two that turns to his advantage.

He threw up his hands. "Okay, you caught me. I can move things around — sometimes, if they're a few ounces. But I haven't been around sunshine for a while."

An opportunity whispered to me. "Do you think you could lift a DVD? Maybe move it a couple inches and push a button?"

"Way out of my league, kid."

I slunk toward a gray metal chair. Does everything have to be hard just because we're not paying taxes anymore? I thought spirits were supposed to be free, unhindered, able to cross continents with the speed of thought and swagger safely through the core of a nuclear reactor whenever the mood strikes us.

But here I was, unable to move a couple of ounces of molded plastic. And more than that: I didn't know my own name for a certainty, my pre-interment background, my hometown. Jeez, I didn't even know my astrological sign.

Fast Eddie sat down beside me. "You don't think this is a stumblie, do you? I mean, is moving a bean such a big deal?"

I shook my head.

"I don't do it because I want to go back to the sunshine," he went on. "It's just that a lot of our folks were in 12-step groups on the Other Side. They practically lived on caffeine. I always thought a nice coffee smell put them in the right frame of mind to talk about recovery."

I looked at him. Fast Eddie's jaw bristled with white whiskers, and his face had the sort of patchy complexion I've always associated with breathers who would be eligible soon for my recovery program. His clothes tended to run to white shirts with soiled collars; he had a wrist watch that had a frayed band and whose hands had, appropriately, stopped; baggy pants with wide cuffs, and a mismatched suit coat that long ago abandoned even the pretence of having a shape.

They say that people end up with the face they deserve, and specters start out with an appearance that matches the way they went through life. If that's the case, I was lucky to get the physical form of a man in his mid-twenties, not the fifth-grader physique I probably deserve. For Fast Eddie, there probably wasn't much difference between his approaches to existence on either side of the Great Divide.

"You were a Tosser," I said.

"I've been known to knock one down in my time. But that's behind me now."

"Cal expects me to do a little outreach with a Tosser. That guy Fergus who showed up a couple nights ago. Maybe you could help."

"No, no, no." He spun his hands as though wiping the idea off the air. "I've never met a Tosser who could be talked into coming here when he's not ready."

"Interesting," I murmured. "I ought to get Cal's opinion about that. Maybe, while I'm at it, ask him whether a spook who's been known to send a coffee bean or two flying should be considered a newbie."

Excessive subtlety has never been a fault of mine, and I was sure Fast Eddie was what we call a *wet brain*, owing to too much embalming fluid at the funeral home. But those wheels started whirling behind his eyes. When it came to figuring out his best interests, I was starting to see Fast Eddie could read the wind better than a dandelion wisp.

He said, "I'd hardly be able to look myself in the mirror —"

"— if you *could* look at yourself in the mirror —"

"— if I wasn't willing to extend the hand of recovery to a still-suffering spook."

"Nicely put."

"When do we start?"

"How about now?"

Fast Eddie's eyes scanned the room. "Well, I don't see much else to do here. Okay, then."

I did my own quick inspection. The coffee bean that rolled under the chair was gone.

Fast Eddie brought me to a section of Broad Street I don't usually go to. Cal would call it one of the *stumblie places*. You know the kind — lit, off the beaten track, deserted by the better class of spooks. In the filmy windows of run-down stores, a specter whose transcendence was in tatters might suddenly appear. His eyes would be sunken, his complexion pale and glowing, his hand outstretched to you, but there's nothing you could give him that he could receive.

These are the ones our literature talks about who are *constitutionally incapable of being dead*. Cal calls them *day trippers*. Sometimes, you can even feel the afternoon heat radiating from them long after midnight.

It's enough to send a deceased entity rushing for the nearest mausoleum.

As we went down the sidewalk, the shrunken figures in the shadows acknowledged Fast Eddie with furtive nods. Some he greeted with a whispered name — Philadelphia Phil, Blue Eyes O'Brien, Dog Turd Frank. This last one bothered me, but, in fairness, I wasn't able to get a good look at him.

At the front of an abandoned, multi-story derelict building surrounded by blocks stripped of everything except tortured earth, we stopped.

"Well, this is the place," Fast Eddie said. "Tossers don't socialize much. But if there's anywhere our boy might show up, it'd be here."

I studied the entrance. There was nothing that says a specter has to use a door, but with a little post-mortality under your belt, most of us can think of reasons we don't want to rematerialize behind an unknown wall. My reasons involve a laundry and a vat of soaking diapers.

The arts department of the college must have taken on the ground floor of this eye-sore as an urban-renewal project. For the bricks and boarded-up windows had been painted to resemble a jungle. A jungle, that is, as seen by a psychotic on acid.

The wide front doors were covered by a single peach whose ultra-bright orange might constitute an assault in some municipalities. In the parade of life on the wall, giraffes were smaller than monkeys, tree trunks wider than rivers, and all the colors had the intensity I associate with the hangovers of my previous life.

"Once we get in there," Fast Eddie said, "there's no telling what we may run into. I might not be able to help you."

I'd been in my share of tough spots: why, I once spent twenty minutes talking to Rosetta. And look at how neatly I'd shaken Gilda from my tail.

I gave him a double thumbs-up, said, "Once more into the peach, good friends," and drifted through the door.

CHAPTER

he building was a war-zone. Beyond the entrance, the floor had collapsed into the basement. I couldn't tell whether this was from gravity or a demolition crew that started gutting the place decades ago and forgot to come back one Monday morning.

Every surface was buried under lumps of shattered concrete, enough to make even the best-behaved Tosser go nuts. They could pitch rocks four or five stories up without drawing the attention of breathers or do-gooders from 12-step groups. And beginners, whose anger at the things of their first lives was, shall we say, unfocused, had plenty of room to practice.

A gleam in the rubble caught my eye; I eased further into the debris field. Above stretched a gigantic hole in the floors that rose a half-dozen flights, suffused by a soft gray light from dust-caked windows filtering the glow of the downtown streetlamps.

A CD lay on top of the refuse. Not a flake of dirt marred its luster. Could a Tosser work with objects other than rocks and stones? Just a few minutes ago, I had seen Fast Eddie lift a coffee bean. He said he couldn't move a DVD, but why should I take a Tosser's word for anything? Besides, I hadn't used all my spectral charm on him.

"Hey, Fast Eddie! Old pal, old friend, old buddy."

But Eddie wasn't there. Had he been waylaid by Philadelphia Phil over an old gambling debt? Or had Dog Turd Frank come up with an entertainment idea too irresistible for Fast Eddie? It didn't matter. I was here and he was not.

The vast cavern of the abandoned store loomed over me like the dome of a medieval cathedral. The CD was a communion host, a sacrament. Surely, there was no sin in a simple act of faith. And what faith could be greater than the belief of a dead man that he was in the here-after for a reason?

Faith. That's what it comes down to. Faith that can move mountains can also move a little, bitty, inconsequential, digital storage disc. After all, I was a child of the cosmos. Why had I allowed myself to surrender my powers — my natural, Uber-spirit-given authority — over the things of all worlds?

Cal and the others in my home-group wouldn't begrudge me the chance to learn about my first life. Wasn't that simply a healthy, inevitable step toward becoming a better citizen of this, my second-life?

Where's the harm in trying?

I concentrated on the gleaming CD. Not knowing what to think, or how this works. Filled with the conviction that force of will was the answer. Confident that, if I could move this CD, I could manage a *Honeymooner's* DVD.

I stared. The CD twinkled innocently. I stared harder.

The CD flew at my face.

It would have been nice to believe, just for a minute or two, that I had some latent powers as a Tosser. That what I already had in the here-after wasn't all that I'd get.

Poor pitiful me. It's the story of my afterlife. No luck in putting the old razzle-dazzle on anyone. Including myself.

I couldn't kid myself. I saw the pebble that hit the edge of the disc and flipped it upward. I glanced through the hole in the floors above. My boy Fergus was glaring down at me.

For an unlucky guy, though, I have my moments.

"Did you do that?" I shouted. "That's an impressive piece of marksmanship. When I think about the hoops a Tosser has to go through to do that, it takes my breath away. Which is, I hope you understand, a figure of speech. Not the best one perhaps, but certainly not my idea of something that would upset a friend."

I shut up to give the kid the opportunity to tell me that no offense was taken. Fergus, as a non-verbal type, had his own way of responding.

A concrete block the size of a cabin cruiser floated into view overhead, and when it dropped, it came like a laser-guided bomb that had the tip of my astral head as its bull's-eye. My experience in the repossessed house had primed my reflexes. I jumped into hyper-transcendental space before the leviathan passed the fourth floor, and by the time it plummeted past the third floor, I was accelerating at a rate that was roughly the speed of light squared.

When that concrete block hit the ground, it rattled the foundations of the building and sent a plume of dust and ash to the ceiling, where it ricocheted downward again, mingled with more aerosolized junk heading for the ceiling and created a vortex of such intensity that the laws of gravity, thermodynamics and supply-and-demand were temporarily suspended.

About a millionth of a second later, I hit the wall that had relocated itself to the area where the front entrance of the building used to be, impacting it with enough force to dislodge dangling wires, loose boards, shattered wallboard or anything else in the building that was unhappy with the status quo.

There's no display of stars for the specter who's *had his bell rung* beyond the Great Divide. No, we're treated to a show of flying Oreo cookies.

This wasn't the time to sort out my misunderstandings with Fergus and convince the poor lad that I was only interested in helping him recover from sunshine. Then again, it's possible that Fergus knew Cal and had a good idea of the lengths to which Cal was willing to put me to bring a suffering specter into the fold.

"If this is a bad time, Fergus, I'd be happy to come back later," I shouted. "I'll just get my old buddy Fast Eddie, who you can't see, seeing how he's standing over there where you can't see him, and we'll leave. The two of us. Me and my witness."

A mad howl shook the building. Beelzebub with a stubbed toe couldn't have sounded so out-of-sorts.

"Then again," I added, "why don't I just scratch your name off my to-do list? You're an adult. You don't need supervision. You can drop by the ol' St. Sears group if there's ever anything we can do for you. You'll always be welcome."

Fergus registered his displeasure by pitching a seven-story stairwell in my direction.

Overhead, the gray light seeping through filthy windows gave the cavern the look of a very large ash tray. Even at a distance, I could make out the shadows of the bars on the windows' exterior. If a ceramic elephant could get me out of a repo house, imagine what a hurtling stairwell could do to a barred window.

I started for the windows. The floor rose up and shook off chunks of concrete and twisted rebar, plus a mountain of plasterboard and a smattering of metal pipes. Then it took a swing at me.

By that I mean exactly what I said. The floor peeled itself from the ground or whatever keeps a floor from aspiring to become a wall, shook itself as though it were a dog emerging from a river, and swung at me like a trap door slamming shut.

Stale air whooshed across my face; plasterboard and dirt peppered my body. I was back in a three-dimensional world, and I didn't like it. My feet scraped across the floor. The wall my hand grabbed for balance was rough, the stench of a million dead things and the accumulated dust of decades clogged my throat.

"EDDIE," I screamed. "I COULD USE A LITTLE HELP IN HERE. NOW WOULD BE A GOOD TIME TO DROP BY."

With a thunderous bellow, the exterior wall tore loose from its foundation and ripped free from the flooring. A gap opened in the corner of the building; and through it, I saw the tired glow of a streetlight by a used book store on the other side of the street where homeless people had gathered to watch.

Before I could move, the wall pivoted like a gate on its hinges to close the gap and plowed through the rest of the structure. Clawing, scrambling, stumbling, I hurried away from the wreckage as debris from each of the building's seven-stories showered down, only to discover I'd been maneuvered into a corner. Sections of flooring mocked me by rising up like gigantic cobras, swaying to the tune of a flute only they could hear; two walls now pulled away from their foundations and swung loose. Across the gutted interior, windows popped free of the walls and prowled the dimness like a pack of very thin, restless, semi-transparent wolverines.

I lunged at the only wall that seemed to be a pacifist and boinked my head hard enough to see another half-pack of Oreos circling around.

Cal always told me the night would come when the only thing keeping me together was the Uber Spirit. He was probably thinking more transcendently, and his notion of *keeping me together* undoubtedly didn't include protection from the rare, physical dismemberment of a spiritual being.

Still, the old boy was on target. Not as well, perhaps, as Fergus, but still making the bull's-eye sweat.

"EDDIE! WHERE ARE YOU? I NEED YOU!"

A hundred feet of electrical wire twisted itself into a noose, and, ambling through the air with a swagger, came at me. Owing to problems of scale, I was able to step through the looped wire, which lassoed a fifteen-foot section of hardwood flooring that was learning to ripple the jagged ends of its boards in a fair replication of the world's first genuine wood saw.

As more of the floor reared up, popping nails along the way, and longer sections of wall circled around me, the situation was passing the point where luck was needed and closing fast upon territory that called for miraculous intervention.

At that moment, Fergus came closer to fitting the description of a deity than anyone else nearby. However, I would rather spend the next thousand centuries squashed inside a thimble than ask for help from a twit who thought it was a big deal to toss pebbles at a roof. Or to wreck a harmless shack by the river that had never done him any harm.

When I thought about it — and I was thinking about it a lot as the building closed in on me — I came to the startling conclusion that I had had a higher power in my first life. I know what it is like to look to someone better, wiser, more powerful than me, someone who can solve all my problems, ease my mind when I am troubled and subject me to righteous discipline when I am a slacker. I even know the name of my higher power.

I call her *woman*.

But where am I going to find a woman in a place like this within the next, ah, let's see, three and a half seconds?

"Okay, what's going on here?" a female voice asked.

With two and a quarter seconds to spare, my prayers were answered.

"I asked a question," the woman's voice said. "Do I have to wait all night for an answer?"

Ducking under a stretch of pipe that was about to impale me to an upended section of floor as though it were a giant staple, I looked for the source of the high-pitched, totally authoritative voice.

Margie stood in the center of the floor. Her gown glowed, her face glowered, and even the speckles of dust near her quit fooling around and quickly landed.

"Boy, am I glad to see you," I said.

I lifted my hand to wave, and my fingers slid through the pipe that had been trying to skewer me.

I was back on the astral plane.

CHAPTER Twelve

'm not sure why it should be so, but the building was creepier once Margie arrived and things calmed down than it had been earlier, when every board, loop of wiring, electrical outlet, toilet lid and drywall fragment was out to get me.

The problem, I guess, was the way the building settled down — the hardwood floors locked into position like waves frozen in an arctic sea; pipes that once aimed at my nose now targeted the dusty air; and the walls, which had broken loose from their foundations, trembled as patrol cars and fire trucks rumbled toward the epicenter of the chaos.

I was thrilled to be back in the normality of the paranormal; I flitted back and forth through walls, lamp posts, trash cans, even the odd cat or two. Margie, like a typical newbie, watched where she stepped while navigating the debris field and slipped through a gap in the walls.

Fast Eddie was toast. Stale, inconsequential, years-old toast when I got my hands on him.

During my first couple of weeks on this side of materiality, I was afraid to lose contact with the surface of the physical world. Put some of that down to force of habit. And let me tell you, walking on solid objects is a tough habit to break. I was concerned about drifting through the ground and not being able to pull up: I even foresaw myself gliding into the molten core of the planet. Or sliding into space and ending up coasting through the bleak, frozen spaces between galaxies for all eternity.

Brrrr. I didn't die for that sort of hardship.

So I didn't protest when Margie insisted on slinking around the side of the old building so the cops wouldn't see us. I was happy to indulge any newbie who could frighten off Fergus.

"How did you do that?" I asked, once we'd put a little distance between us and the wailing sirens.

"Do what?"

"Get that demented spook to leave me alone."

The question perplexed her, which perplexed me, but I reminded myself that she was a newcomer. Gotta give the kid a little room to grow into her new home. She might be here for a very long time.

I said, "Forget that I asked."

She shook her head, and gold sparkled when the faint light touched her hair. "I thought that evil ghost was making fun of me. Isn't that just like a woman? It's always about me."

"What made you think the spook inside that building was making fun of you?"

"Not him," she rushed on. "I'm talking about the other gentleman outside the building. The one who tried to scare me from coming inside, even though I heard your voice and you were calling for help."

"Yeah, imagine that." I kicked the husk of a rusty soup can and, naturally, whisked out the other side. "This guy who wasn't treating you so well – how would you describe him?"

"I don't want to be unkind."

"Then let me try. Did he look like a dirty-clothes basket that could walk itself to the cleaners, if it ever took a fancy to do that?"

Margie nodded reluctantly.

Fast Eddie. I looked around. This part of downtown looked like a wasteland. Behind us, more emergency vehicles had arrived, joined by the bright lights of a film crew, although I couldn't tell whether that was Margie's Hollywood team or the folks from one of the local TV channels.

Lights, camera, but no action from Fast Eddie, a spineless representative of the recovering community who led a brother spook to a repo building and abandoned him. Then there was Fergus, who committed the unheard of crime of attacking a fellow specter.

76

I told Margie, "I was lucky that you happened to come along –"

"It's no big thing, really."

"– arriving in the nick of time –"

"You're making too much of this. Please. "

"– exactly where I needed you."

"Nothing, really."

"In the middle of an abandoned building, in the worst section of the city, alone."

Margie slowed down, a hitch came to her walk. Head down, brow creased, she studied the earth with great care, absorbed in her exploration of tufts of dying grass and tar paper shingles dissolving into the earth.

"I know people who've been dead for two hundred years who won't go within a half mile of that place," I added.

Her lip – the lower one, the exquisite one – trembled. "You think I'm following you. You think I'm a terrible woman."

No, I think you're a mal-adjusted spook is what I wanted to say. Instead, ever the diplomat, I opted for: "I'm very glad you were there tonight. I've never before felt like a damsel in distress."

"And I've never felt like Sir Lancelot."

That broke the chill. We continued to walk silently side-by-side toward the river; a companionable aura lay between us.

As we crossed Floyd Avenue, Margie glanced at me and, this time, she wasn't in a hurry to break the contact.

Instead, she said, "It really was luck that put me in that building when you needed a friend. But as for why I was in the area, I was doing research. For my role in the movie, where I'm supposed to be playing a ghost. I had heard that people considered that old building – I know you're going to think now that I'm hopelessly silly – but they said it was haunted."

"Naw." I wasn't exactly sure what *incredulity* meant, but I did my darndest to overflow with it. "So, you wanted to find out what ghosts look like and how they sound and what happens when they move things."

"Well, yes." It was a very polite *Well, yes*. "What I really want to do is get inside a ghost's head."

"Easier for one of them to get inside yours."

"Pardon?"

"I said, it's easier if you pretend to be dead. Then you'd be able to spy on them."

"You're right. You're exactly right." Margie spun around and headed back the way we'd come. "If I'm ever going to understand ghosts, I've got to spy on them. See the world through their sheets. Understand what makes them . . . er . . . groan."

I hurried after her. "You're not going back in that building? It's not safe."

"I have to. It's my job." Determination settled on her face. "If it floats like a ghost and moans like a ghost and is invisible like a ghost, it must be a ghost."

Necessity may be the mother of invention, but desperation runs a sixteen-wheel mobile ob-gyn clinic.

"I had a crazy aunt," I said, working this out as I went along. "She had extrasensory powers. She could communicate with the dead and look into their world."

"What did she see?" Margie's pace slowed.

"Mostly she saw the basements of churches. Spooks gather each night to talk about their feelings. They're helping each other to make the change from a breather to a specter."

"Meetings in church basements," she mused. "Just like the meeting you took me to."

"Why, I hadn't thought of that," I said. "What a coincidence."

"It sounds like a 12-step program."

By this time, I'd maneuvered her into heading back toward the river. "Exactly. Dead people are still people. Their bodies may be rotting in some hole in the ground, but they still have feelings."

Her smile was bright enough to pose a threat to any spook. "I like your attitude."

"You don't have to hang around moldy bodies and collapsing buildings to know what to do," I protested. "Help Hollywood create a vision of the afterlife that's worth dying for. Get beyond those clichés of doors slamming shut, and cold draughts on the stairs, and people disappearing in creepy houses."

"And walls that try to grab people," she was getting her color back. "And floors that try to stomp people. And, what was that thing that was trying to get you at the end?"

"A water pipe."

"Yeah, no more water pipes strangling people in the films. Let's be absolutely honest about what ghosts are like." Margie was getting fired up. "People appreciate honesty. Hollywood needs to show more dead people in recovery. Let's take the *cover* off of recovery and see what we've got left."

"Wouldn't that leave you with an *R-E* and then a *Y*?" I asked.

"And what does that spell? That spells *hope!*"

If I had any breath, it would have been taken away by the vision of Margie, fists clenched, shoulders square and back fishing-rod straight (*I know it's supposed to be* ramrod *straight, but I don't know what a* ramrod *is, although I can certify that a fishing rod is pretty straight. Now, where was I? Oh:*) fishing-rod straight as she marched across the barren field to the sirens and the blindingly glaring camera lights by the building that was collapsing upon itself.

I turned and kept heading toward the river. For me, all directions lead toward the water. Barely two blocks from Broad Street, the ground had been chewed up by heavy construction equipment, and the scent of diesel fuel lingered in the air.

Besides an obvious sense of stupefaction, I felt rather good. Fast Eddie had dragged me into the astral version of the House on Elm Street, but I was still okay. Fergus the Tosser had eluded me again, but on the other hand, I had eluded him, which to my mind more than balanced the scales. Then there was Margie, whom I'd nudged ever-so discreetly to quit denying her own status as a decedent.

I'll admit to feeling a slight twinge about Gilda because she felt I was neglecting her. Well, it was a twinge that was going to be coming sooner or later. Next to Margie, Gilda was just another storm cloud with chains.

My mood was so good that seeing Edgar Allan Poe rise up from the shadows of a magnolia with a dark bird perched on his shoulder didn't change it. Not immediately.

"Nevermore," Edgar A- said with his high-pitched voice which didn't know whether to twang, drawl or flow.

I veered toward him. He didn't seem prepared to have a fellow specter do anything other than flee.

From force of habit, he began: "Once upon a midnight dreary, while I pondered weak and weary —"

"I know, I know," I said, giving him a close toes-to-head inspection, with a detour to take in the raven on his shoulder. That bird was definitely fishing-rod straight. In fact, it bobbled when he moved.

"Your bird," I said, pointing.

"What about my bird?"

"He's dead."

"No, he's not."

I waved my hand inches from the raven's eyes. They didn't blink.

"Dead," I insisted.

"No." Edgar A- regarded the area around his scuffed black boots. "He's just over-medicated. He'll be fine. Give him a few minutes to shake it off."

"He's got all the time in this world. He's dead."

"Ah, I can see why you say that. It's his thyroid. He just doesn't have the old get up and go."

"His *get up and go* is now his *lie down and be gone*. He's dead, I tell you."

Edgar A- stared into the motionless glass eyes inches from his nose. "He's meditating, is what's happening. Listen, can't you hear him humming his mantra?"

I stomped into the night to my meeting. Sometimes I wonder what made me think the sunshine-life was so interesting.

CHAPTER Thirteen

efore I got to the church, I heard the shouting a half-block away. A group of fellow sufferers joined together in recovery, guided by time-tested principles, each possessing a desire to help and be helped, and all committed to transcendence – Let me tell you, that can be an explosive mix.

Rosetta and Hank were outside on the stoop.

"Such language," Rosetta wheezed. "How can you inspire recovery in the newly arrived by talking as if you were a"– Rosetta was reaching here, and sensing she was on the verge of casting off all self-control, I zipped closer –"a sanitation engineer?"

"I call them like I see them," Hank said, the little pony-tail at the back of his head and his single gold earring nodding in agreement.

"But can't you see things from a gentler perspective?"

"What's gentle about being *planted?* That happened to all of us. And that's all I said."

Rosetta smiled a sickly smile. "*Interment.* Doesn't that sound nicer than being treated like a daffodil?"

"Daffodils don't get smothered in hooey."

Rosetta wailed so loudly I'm sure spooks along the East Coast must be shaking their heads and wondering who's tormenting a cat.

I slipped around her and went inside through the wall.

Darleen and Cal were having a more civilized disagreement on one of the finer points of the program. Something to do with how much sunshine a spook in recovery can absorb — inadvertently — before it qualifies as the sort of reboot moment that we call *a stumblie*.

"The *Teeny Book* says we've put our bright, sunshiny ways behind us," Darleen averred.

Cal gave her a look reserved by breathers for crazed Sumo wrestlers. "That's exactly what I'm saying. That spook supports our program. He likes the idea of being dead: it really cuts down on his expenses. He doesn't want to be a breather again."

"Then how do you explain the sun tan?"

"An accident. It could happen to anybody. He didn't know it was a tanning bed. Why give the kid a lot of grief. He feels awful already. Worse than the night he woke up in a funeral home."

"That's fine, then. We're agreed."

"Fine. I'm glad you finally came to your senses."

"If he stumbles into the sunshine like a newbie, then he *is* a newbie."

Much as I enjoy a good circus, especially when Cal is in the center ring and he isn't over-taxing his voice in my direction, I eased out of his line of sight. He has a tendency during moments of stress to put the spooks he sponsors — we call them *ravens* — through a week-long series of lectures on the origins, philosophy and underlying science of the Specters Anonymous program.

In a corner of the room, trying to slink through a bookcase, was a figure that somebody recently had identified as a walking bag of dirty laundry.

"Not so fast there, Eddie."

Fast Eddie had a world-class slink, but the way the other arguments in the room died down when I shouted at him appealed to his higher instinct. I'm talking about his instinct to look good at all costs.

"Ralph, my boy!" He was again the model of good cheer and brotherly concern. "You're back. Oh, my. I can't tell you what a relief this is."

"I'll bet you can't."

"That old wreck of a building has never acted like a repo before." He was now talking for the benefit of Cal and Hank and Darleen. "The instant you went inside, I followed you through the wall and — *bang* — the wall was solid. Has anyone ever heard of repossessed property turning on a dime?"

"Repos aren't the only things that change sides without warning," I offered.

Low level pandemonium returned to the room. Rosetta and Mrs. Hannity got into a contest to see who had the worst repo story, Cal demanded that I explain what I meant by that crack about *changing sides*, and Fast Eddie started easing back into the bookcase.

"So, what exactly did you do to help me?" I screamed at Fast Eddie. "I'm stuck in a repo, you knew it, nobody else knew it, and your response was what?"

"Everybody knows repossessed property is dangerous for us spooks. You don't want to be caught dead in one of those places."

"But I'm already dead. And I was in one of those places. Because you took me there and left me."

By now, I had the full attention of the group, which was, to my best recollection, the first time that ever happened, including the nightly meetings when I spoke.

Fast Eddie was caught off guard – another first – and unable to conceal his puzzlement.

"I'm a ghost, too, kid. What do you expect me to do?"

"How about opening the door? It was, after all, a repo, and we can do that with a repo. What kept you from coming inside and seeing if you could help me?"

I may never know whether Fast Eddie was tongue-tied because he hadn't thought about taking such a simple, natural action, or because he couldn't think of an alibi fast enough.

In the awkward moment as a room full of specters saw Fast Eddie stutter and fumble for an explanation, Cal pointed at me and said, "You, come with me." Hank got the same finger and the same message.

Cal took Hank and me over the streets and buildings at *flank speed*, which is somewhere on the spectral speedometer between a walk and a thunderbolt.

"What was that with Fast Eddie?" he asked.

"That spook let me down," I said. "Big time."

"And that surprised you?"

The question caught me off guard, and I realized I wasn't going to be getting any sympathy for my latest tussle with Fergus. Eddie didn't earn the nickname *Fast* because of his gentle, thoughtful ways with his fellow spooks.

"Shouldn't we be tracking down that Tosser?" I asked, deflectingly.

"Yep," Cal said.

A couple dozen things to say came to mind in the space of three seconds, most ending with the phrase, *Then what in the Roth are we doing up here?* Hank looked entirely too eager for me to open my mouth, so I let the moment pass.

"Whatever happened to that spook who came in the other night?" Cal said. "The one with all the black leather and attitude?"

"Gilda?" I answered. "She's around here somewhere."

"Don't you think she might appreciate a little help fitting into the afterlife?"

I didn't see that question coming. I didn't even see that idea on the horizon. Gilda was as rock-solid as anything in the astral world gets. She was beyond the normal range of insecurities and fears. Maybe it was the black leather and purple fingernails. Finding out that she was, after all, a veteran of the afterlife, not a newbie, wouldn't make much of a difference when Cal started putting together a list of projects for me.

Cal, however, spoke so seldom that he didn't know that questions are supposed to be followed by answers.

"Have I ever talked to you boys about transcendence?" He had this way of boring through you without turning his face in your direction, and I felt as though I was having an encounter with an astral auger.

"Yes, sir, you've mentioned it," I answered.

"Did you ever," Hank said, giving my shoulder a prod with his elbow. "Old Cal doesn't listen to himself much, does he?"

"The question is how much you hear," Cal said.

Richmond slid below us. Amid the sickly street lamps downtown, a blaze of flashing, pulsing, twirling lights lit up the hulk of a nine-story building that had lost even the most casual familiarity with the phrase *structural integrity*.

I pointed at the soon-to-be wreckage and said to Cal, "Do you know what happened there? Let me tell you about it."

"I already know. Idiots held a convention there tonight."

My pride was snuffed out before it could properly flicker. In full sulk, I followed Cal as he banked over the James and brought us down just inside the wrought-iron gates of Hollywood Cemetery. I overheard a discussion once between a couple of breathers — a local and a tourist — about why the city's ancient cemetery had the same name as the nation's film capital. *It's because those damned Californians wanted to steal the glamour of Richmond's Hollywood*, the local huffed.

I'm not sure *glamour* was the right word, but Richmond's Hollywood has an excess of atmosphere. Within a compact area of undulating hills and corkscrewing roads was a collection of mausoleums, statues, crypts, columbaria, gravesites and obelisks, plus man-sized urns, Doric pillars and carved angels on stone porticoes in the hillsides that should have signs reading, *Greek Chorus Wanted. Inquire Within.*

One of the advantages of spookdom — right up there with the liberal dress code and decriminalization for Peeping Toms — is our immunity from the weather. Neither rain nor sleet nor boiling heat of summer makes any impression upon us. Cemeteries are another matter.

A cool breeze rose from the ground as if air conditioners were going full bore behind every headstone. I expected to see my breath come out in icy puffs; but, of course, seeing as how Cal, Hank and I, despite our gruff exteriors, are officially breathless, that isn't going to happen.

"I'm surprised you brought me back here," I told Cal.

"Your education in denial is about to move to the graduate level," he said.

"What about my education in finding Tossers?"

"Pay attention."

Cal and Hank drifted up a winding road lined with headstones the size of motorhomes, while I lagged behind to figure out my strange sense of unease. What's to be uneasy about? Everywhere I turned, I saw cheerfully chiseled epitaphs, hand-carved angels and headstones that listed the rank and medals of old soldiers who died a half century after taking off their uniforms.

So why did this place send shivers down my ectoplasmic spine? Then, of course, I answered my own question. I flashed to that instant after leaving the here-after's inprocessing center when I stepped through an ordinary door and found myself in the middle of the interstate outside Richmond as a sixteen-wheeler with a full load of soft drinks roared up my lane.

Much as I like Dr. Pepper, there's something about four or five hundred cans zipping through your body that takes away the magic.

Sometime during those first nights, I ended up at Hollywood Cemetery, going from headstone to headstone. I was looking for the name *Ralph*, and on those rare occasions I actually found one, I would loiter for hours to stare at the last name, the chiseled dates, epitaphs both clichéd and heart-wrenching, the meager details of a life.

Cal had found me before I could visit every headstone in search of the remains of my former, tactile self.

Hurrying up the road after Cal and Hank, I drank in the ambience of the place. And, okay, if from time to time my eyes strayed to an occasional headstone, looking for a certain name in stone, what was the harm?

"Where you been, stranger?"

Jedediah was sitting on a headstone beyond the first curve in the road. His features were almost lost in the darkness, for he was little more than a fine mist. Still, I could make out the imposing beard, a nose remarkable for both its length and its thinness, the high collar of his coat, the elaborate bow tie that covered half his neck, the eyes sunken by his long vigil.

Jedediah was the first spook I met in happily-ever-after. He looked after me until Cal came along. He was a spook who'd actually found his grave, and he could no more leave it than an alcoholic could walk away from a bar at happy hour.

"I'm still doing the 12-step shuffle," I answered, wriggling my feet in a pantomime jig. "You ought to try it."

Jedediah's laugh was no more than a rustle in a pile of dead leaves. "Malcolm up in section twenty-three says they're going to reopen some graves in this area any day now. Something about something called DNA and an influenza that carried off a fair number of folks after the war."

The war was the Civil War, and Malcolm's tale about disinterments was old when I first wandered through here.

"You're still thinking about climbing into that coffin?"

"Where else is a body to go?" Jedediah gave me a look that, in a breather, I might connect to a sudden urge to find a restroom. "Where's a body to go. Get it? *A body.*"

"But you're a spook, Jedediah. If you stay with your body, you'll rot with your body. But if you accept the afterlife of a specter, who knows what will happen to you?"

"Who knows? That's my point, young man. You can't tell me where it'll all end if I get involved in your recovery fiddle-faddle." He snuffed. "Nope, I was born with the body that's here, and I'll stay with it."

"Try just one meeting. Half a meeting. I promise I'll get you out of there at half-time."

Even as a mist, Jedediah put a formidable set to his jaw and took to watching a small animal scurry through the grass on the other side of the road.

"I believe," he said with icy aloofness, "your friends are waiting up ahead for you."

The best way to help a tomb-squatter, Cal always said, *is to keep anyone from becoming a tomb-squatter.*

CHAPTER

s I trudged along the winding path, five or six specters lingering at their gravesites materialized in different parts of the cemetery. Jedediah was among the most time-worn, but I think there were a few older fellows in the colonial section. I'm uncertain because, with the antiques, you have trouble telling them apart from ground fog.

When Cal signaled for me and Hank to join him after the meeting, I was afraid that I'd ignored one of the many suggestions that litter the twelve steps to recovery like ragweed in a wet summer. For once, though, Cal's focus on working with newcomers had slipped, and I was getting anxious about working on Fergus. Preferably with a blunt object just as soon as I'd figured out a way to swing one.

Up ahead, Hank stood on the road alone. Even when he was motionless and silent, Hank gave off the aura of a spook who didn't know the meaning of *ghostly*. Ghostly meant subtle, subdued, understated. Hank was a wrecking machine in ectoplasm who was still trying to find a way to break things.

"Where's Cal?" I asked.

"He went off with a tomb-squatter to look at the guy's left-overs."

"You mean, *remains?*"

"Whatever."

Hank's put-your-head-down-and-hit-the-wall approach to language was one of his endearing traits. Also one of his exasperating qualities.

"Did you ever think," I asked, "whether *Hank* is your real name?"

"Why should I do that?"

"To find out who you really are."

"Who I really am is me. You got a problem with that?"

"No, no. Just wondering."

I gazed across the well-tended lawns. One of the tomb-squatters kept raising his hand to his mouth, then lowering it, and I finally figured out the spook thought he was smoking. After a while, I saw him knock some ash that wasn't there into an ash-tray that wasn't there, either.

Who am I to say he's not actually lighting up? I am, after all, an immaterial being who, a few hours ago, helped wreck a multi-story building. And I've been driven out of my modest home by the river by another immaterial being who just happens to retain the ability to grasp rocks. Maybe Jedediah has the right idea. There's something Zen-like in committing yourself to doing nothing through eternity, transcendent in the belief that some grave-robber or excavator will happen to lift the lid of your casket. At which time, you intend to scoot inside and molder quietly away.

I looked at Hank. "If you found your grave, would you stay there?"

"What kind of question is that? Do I look like a chump? I mean, do I?"

"It's just a question, Hank. Calm down."

"You want I should start asking you questions? Like what you see in that fruitcake Gilda? Or why you're being taken in by Fast Eddie."

The jab at Gilda didn't surprise me. But Fast Eddie? I wasn't interested in defending him, but there are limits even to grudges.

"What do you mean *taken in* by Fast Eddie? What's to be taken in about? After that stunt he pulled – bringing me to a repo, then floating away – Fast Eddie isn't taking me anywhere."

Hank hitched up his belt and gave me plenty of time to realize my words might be outpacing my ability to endure pain. I eyed him coolly and told myself that the dismemberment of my transcendent being could be a learning opportunity from which I could grow – with a special emphasis upon new limbs. Fortunately, Cal came floating around a corner.

Cal needed only a glance to take a reading of the temperature between Hank and me.

"That's enough of that," he said. "I want you boys to come with me."

"What's the haps, chief?" Hank asked.

"The two of you need to see what happens when dead men think they can stay stupid in this life, too."

Faster than the flick of a bat's wing, Cal brought us to the edge of the cemetery. The hillside here was steep, and the front of a mausoleum built into the hill overlooking the river had the gray, time-worn dignity of a relic from a lost civilization.

Poured concrete had been used to fashion pillars, broad steps and the walls on which dead lichen clung like scabs. It was the coldest place I'd been in the afterlife; a sense of foreboding leached from the ashen cement.

"I couldn't agree with you more, chief," Hank said. "Whoever paid good money for this crap deserves everything that happens to them in our world."

"Ralph?" Cal eyed me with his give-it-your-best-shot look.

Beyond the mausoleum, I could see Jedediah, for one of the few times since I'd known him, floating outside the boundaries of his grave. He was in the road and watching us.

I closed my eyes and tried to clear my mind. No more images of buildings collapsing like poorly constructed Legos, no waifs in white gowns or Goths in black leather or Tossers hefting their stones. My thoughts, I was about to tell myself, were as clean as a psychopath's conscience when, from the cul-de-sacs of my mind waddled the image of a bundle of brown, black and white fur, ears and tongue flapping in three different directions at once and brown eyes that no one would dare disappoint.

Why the thought of that beagle should appear at that moment was as mysterious as the calming effect it had on me. I relaxed enough to hear a strange murmur bobbing on the wind. A wave of voices rose from behind the mausoleum's ancient facade, a dozen or more voices, all competing to be heard.

I went closer to the door. It was fashioned of bronze, green with age, pitted by the seasons, but secured by a sparkling new padlock.

"Are you getting the message, Ralph?" Cal asked with a smidgen of gentleness.

Slowly, tentatively, I put my hand to the door. My fingertips had barely sunk into the old metal before I felt a strange sensation on my skin — warm and tingly, like miniature squids probing my knuckles and palm. I jerked back; the invisible squids clamped down on my fingers. Had I reacted a fraction of second later I would have been pulled inside.

As it was, I jumped back and rolled down the steps, down the hill and into the road.

Hank snickered.

I rose and brushed away the dust that wasn't on my hands. "Well, that turned out exactly the way I planned."

A tomb-squatter came over from the other side of the road where he'd been loitering on a headstone with flowers and lambs carved around the sides. He wore a crushed, narrow-brimmed hat, and the sort of pants that only came down to his knees. A ghostly baseball bat rested on his shoulder.

"It's like I told this other gentleman," he said, indicating Cal. "Couple nights ago, a strange fellow showed up. One of us croakers. Never seen him before. He was pacing up and down in front of the place across the road like it had the last privy in Richmond and he'd just left a beer-drinking contest."

"What did he look like?" I asked.

"You know what a cemetery worker looks like, one of those fellows who does the digging? Big boots all caked with clay, dirt on his hands, sweat stains on his back?"

Cal nodded. "I know the type."

"Well, he didn't look nothing like that."

"But what did he look like?" I repeated.

"You know those police"– he pronounced it *POE-lees* –"forensics experts? With fancy gloves and a coat that looks like he'd been jerking sodas all day? Narrow in the waist and in the chest, arms like rake handles, squinty eyes?"

"I got the number," Hank said.

"That's not the type, either."

I felt my ectoplasm rise. "But what did he look like?"

Cal raised a hand and said, "I expect this fellow didn't look anything like a grave-robber."

The spook somberly nodded. "That's a fair description."

"Anything unusual about the spook?"

"Well, he did have something you don't see every night on a specter," the squatter said, looking back at his gravesite anxiously. "Tattoos. All up and down his arms."

"Fergus," I whispered.

Cal kept his focus on the squatter. "Tell my friends what he did."

"He went up the hill to section seventeen, where old Lou Roughtan's been camping out since before Lindy landed in Paris. Darned if that tattooed fellow didn't come back with Lou. They had some words – pleasant enough, but the stranger must have put a first-class shine on Lou. I knowed that because old Lou ended up walking straight into the mausoleum."

"The stranger spent the better part of the night talking to him through the door, then ended up bedding down in a woodpecker hole near the forked branches of the oak over there. You look close, even in this light, you can see where the trunk got split by a lightning bolt in '37. Or was it '38?"

"Then what happened?" Cal asked, with patience made possible because he doesn't waste any compassion on the likes of me.

"Next night, before the sun properly sets, he's back. This time with another croaker. Gives him the shine. In the spook goes through the door. Only this time, the fellow only talks to him for an hour or so. Guess he wasn't as interesting as old Lou.

"Off he goes again. Then back he comes, this time with a lady decedent. And, boy, does the flimflam fly. I can tell just by looking at her. He gets her to that old brass door like a fine lord escorting the queen of England to her potty. She goes through the door, he talks, then listens. Then, out of respect for the fairer sex, I suppose, he floats like he's sitting on the stairs. I can hear her blessing him like he was all the saints and prophets.

"Three, four, maybe five more times that night, the same dang stuff kept happening. If this were a book-story, I might be bored by then. But it weren't and I wasn't. Only thing was, by the time the last croaker eyes that door, the east was starting to light up and the spook with the tats shoved the last arrival through the door."

"What do you make of it?" Cal asked.

"Reckon patience wasn't that spook's strong suit."

Hank stepped in front of the tomb-squatter. "That's not what the man asked."

The old fellow stepped back, gave his bat a couple of level swings, and I think Hank remembered that he can sneer all he wants at a real baseball bat. But a spook's bat will have him seeing flying Oreo cookies in no time.

CHAPTER Fifteen

That night, I learned that Cal, a man who could put a razor's edge on a preposition or make the most casual shrug hit you like an exploding volcano, was one of the legendary *ghost whisperers*.

He could talk a rampaging poltergeist into setting down its skillets and flower pots to take a little nap, or coax a terrified newbie to step deeper into a dark, rat-infested cave and not into the sunshine.

Half the night, Cal floated near the brass door of that mausoleum and talked softly and listened and nodded with such sympathy that the frightened spooks inside should have linked arms and burst into campfire songs.

But the here-after isn't a perfect world, either. The poor souls knew they shouldn't have let that sweet-talking deceiver Fergus wheedle them into somebody else's tomb, knowing full well they wouldn't be able to get out unassisted. So they stayed scared, and Cal's magic was wasted on the cemetery air. But maybe not. When Cal slunk back to the road, his head hanging low and his astral feet dragging above the grass, Hank took his place at the door.

For a couple of hours, Hank stood there and serenaded the night with lullabies. Who'd have thought my buddy Hank knew how to carry a tune in an urn? I saw a spider scurry down its web to lift a filament so as not to endanger a moth, rabbits squatted shoulder-to-shank with a fox and twitched their tails in time to the melodies, a bat crashed into an oak trunk lest it disturb the flight path of an extended mosquito family.

Sunrise was three-quarters of an hour away when Hank stepped aside. He was getting hoarse, but the issue wasn't that his voice was losing its timbre but that his singing was so mournful that the turtles were in danger of dehydration from weeping.

Once Hank joined us on the road, the mausoleum stoop was empty in an accusatory manner. Cal pursed his lips and looked away. Hank pursed his lips and looked away. I pursed my lips and stepped forward.

Cal had tried gentle cajoling, Hank offered songs from the cradle. What was left? Fear came quickly to my mind, but there's only so much terror you can inflict upon someone whose last visit to a dentist was years ago.

I leaned toward the brass door. "You guys comfortable in there?"

Six or eight spooks responded at once, and I knew from watching Cal that it was useless to try persuading them to be reasonable. Only one road — according to my sense of navigation — seemed untaken.

"Could you pick up the volume a bit?" I asked. "Don't worry about how it's going to sound. No need to agree on the lyrics. Just let it all out. Let's hear you guys give a scream that'll wake the living. Let's hear a good one for old Hollywood Cem."

It was tough to tell, what with the rabbits and the fox still twitching their tails and the crickets picking up the rhythm, but I thought the ruckus inside the tomb dropped a notch or two.

"I'm supposed to keep this a secret," I continued, "but there's this new reality show, *Great American Cemetery Choruses*, and their producer is wandering through section thirty-nine right now. You know what that means, huh? Can't you hear opportunity when it comes knocking on your sepulcher?"

I listened. I pretended to rap on the door three times.

"I'm just a spook," I went on, "who thinks the theme from *The Addams Family* is one of the world's great artistic achievements. But hearing you folks wail away, I think you might have it. I'm not talking about just any old *it*. But the sort of *it* that can reach right into a hole in the ground and pull out"— dramatic pause here —"a star!"

For three or four glorious seconds, the mausoleum was silent. The wind skittered through the leaves overhead. I heard a sixteen-wheeler out on the Boulevard Bridge down-shifting. Somewhere in Carytown a CD was playing *Louie, Louie* for the four hundredth time.

I moved as close to the door as I dared. This shouldn't be complicated.

"A spook named Fergus talked you into going into this mausoleum." I said. "What did he say? Maybe we can help you if we get an idea how this all happened. I want one spook – whoever's closest to the door right now – to talk to me."

For the first time, a single voice was clear and distinct.

"Closest to the door, you say? That would be me."

I almost jumped into the tomb to hug her. "Yes, lady, you're the one. Talk to me."

A second voice, young, male and whiny, arose. "Wait a minute. He said he wanted a spook. You've been telling us since the moment you got here that you're not one of us."

"But I'm not. I would never use that despicable word to describe myself."

"*Spook* isn't despicable. You'd probably take objection to being called a miserable old scum-bag, too."

And they were off to the races again. I tried to tempt them into silence with lies about the producer from the other Hollywood, but apparently the specters inside the tomb, having had a couple minutes to rest their voices, were determined to hit new peaks of chaos.

Cal led me from the door once a lighter shade of gray began to appear in the east.

"Maybe we'll try again tomorrow night," he said.

"I see what you meant earlier about learning about denial," I told him. "All this wreckage and misery from one spook who doesn't know the meaning of *dead*."

Cal answered with a nod.

I cast a wishful look behind. This was supposed to be the moment when the door crashes open, or the gaggle of specters inside goes quiet long enough for a single voice to rise above the racket with a decisive piece of information, or a slip of paper with a cryptic clue slides beneath the bronze door.

But the mausoleum entrance, with its pretensions of grandeur, stared silently back at me. The morning twilight revealed curlicues of molded cement edging the sides of the facade, and for the first time, I noticed the mock leaves of concrete above the door, and letters rising from a cement wreath.

"S-O-U-I-R-E-S." I squinted. "What is that? French?"

Hank punched my shoulder. "That's not an O. That's a Q."

"Squires," Cal read.

"Squires." The name made me uneasy. "I heard that name not too long ago."

Luckily for detective fiction, Sherlock Holmes didn't have to hurry home each morning before sunrise lest he dissolve into a random assembly of spectral atoms. On instinct, I went back to the shack on the island, only to find a large collection of stones and rocks lying around my flattened and splintered ex-shack.

It seems Fergus – and not a doubt remained in my noggin that this was Fergus's work – was a busy little spook. The old boy made such fast work of conning a bunch of spooks to take a one-way trip into someone else's resting place that he had enough time for his rock-chucking exercise program, using my poor shack for target practice.

What had I ever done to that Tosser? I hadn't known him long enough to start a really memorable grudge. That must mean my grudge-making prowess has become so second-nature-ish that I'm not aware of what I'm doing. Not a healthy development for a spook in recovery whose 12-step program has the motto: *To thine own current self be true.*

But daylight dallies for no specter. In fact, Hank once was at a meeting in the west end where they were moaning about losing one of their regulars when the rotation of the earth sped up to grab this spook in the open because he liked the quiet moments before sunrise.

Normally, I'll brush off a story like that, but when you've started your night being chased by snapping floorboards and end it listening to idiots wailing from inside somebody else's mausoleum, your idea of the plausible gets flexible.

This was the sort of night that can only be dealt with by climbing into a nice dark bucket and giving creation twelve hours to straighten itself out.

For want of a better idea, I headed to the townhouse on the river where Gilda took me yesterday.

From the curved road of Hollywood Cemetery by the James River to the old coffee pot on the dining room wall is a course I had no trouble navigating. But after seeing the mess that a bunch of spooks got into because they assumed they could float out of anything, I materialized on the sidewalk outside the townhouse, scoped out the neighborhood for signs of Fergus or hidden tombs, then went in through the front door.

Too many lights downstairs for my comfort. The hiss of an irritated cobra came from the living room, along with a strange glow. Crinkly the light was – I couldn't explain the word to myself, but I knew it was right.

The beagle met me at the door to the living room with a single, sharp bark, followed by low moaning. Her tail thrashed from one side to the other so violently I was afraid the dog's spine would be thrown out of alignment. I held my hand inches from the animal's shoulders and back, which the beagle treated like the best rub she'd had in years.

"How're you doing, girl? Looks like somebody's got a home."

Slipping into the room, I found the source of both the hissing and the peculiar light. A television set was tuned to a channel that had quit broadcasting, and, without a signal, the set was left with a splotchy white screen and a razzing hiss.

A head wedged into the folds of a pillow on the sofa was aimed at the hissing white screen, while below it stretched the torso, legs and stockinged feet of a sleeping man. I tried to get closer, but the socks stopped me. How can you explain why the population of the western world, after a busy day on their feet, ends up with socks that smell like a three-month-old corpse in its Slumber Rest casket?

Easing from the stench, I drifted to the TV and I saw the box with *The Honeymooner's* DVD collection, opened, with a disc missing. Good thing I was dead, or I would have had a heart attack.

I squatted and squinted, maneuvered and shifted until I could peer over the lip of the DVD player's tray, and while I wasn't willing to bet everything I'd ever owned that the disc was in there, I was probably willing to bet everything someone else owned.

The beagle followed my antics with a sort of sisterly concern.

I lowered myself through the floor until we were practically nose-to-snout. "You're a very smart dog, aren't you?"

The animal's look told me she was surprised I'd ask such a silly question.

"I'll bet you've been punching buttons your entire life. Probably taught button-punching at your obedience school."

A twist of the beagle's head let me know the dog wasn't sure how much more of the leash to give me: she wasn't going to put up with me sniffing around her forever.

"Okay," I said. "Here's the situation. I'd be deeply indebted to you if you'd touch that glowing red button on the machine with the tip of your nose. Nothing too strenuous."

The dog looked over her shoulder at the sleeping man. I stuck my hand under her nose and, having gotten her attention, swept my arm until a finger was pointing at the button in question.

The dog looked at the button. Since she was a good dog, a very good dog, such a pretty dog, she fixated on the button. But neither pleading, promises of a lifetime supply of New York strip steaks, groveling nor careful explanations about my suspicion that the DVD held some secrets about my first life made the slightest impression upon my could-be canine benefactor.

The quality of your transcendence, Cal said, *will be seen most clearly on your worst nights, not your best*. At that moment, I felt I was beyond all that. Beyond transcendence, beyond the imperative not to go floating through the afterlife with a moan on my lips, and especially beyond the prime directive, which commands us to refrain from acting like ghosts just because we happen to be dead.

Besides, the warm brown eyes of the beagle held such compassion and trust. Would I abuse such tender-heartedness merely for a chance that I might learn something about my first life? Was I that kind of a spook?

"BLAAAAHHHH!" I screamed and wiggled my hands in the air.

The beagle jumped back with a wail as though she'd seen . . . well . . . a ghost. Backward she skittered across the hardwood floor, knocked the coffee table hard enough to topple a glass of water, bumped against the sofa and whacked the man with her tail when he tried to sit up.

He lifted the dog and made room for her on the cushions. "You having nightmares, Petey? Maybe seeing mean old dog-catchers in your dreams? You don't have to worry about them anymore. You're our sweetie Petey now. Yes, you are."

Meanwhile, if concentration could move mountains, I would have shoved this dolt into orbit. I fixed on him my best, I'm-dead-so-you-better-be-afraid-of-me look and, adopting the ghost whisperer tone Cal used earlier in the evening, went to work.

"You are growing alert," I murmured. "Very alert. You can feel energy flowing through your fingers, your toes, your ears. You are alive, you are energized. You don't want sleep. Sleep is bad. Sleep is where cooties grow." Sometimes, I must admit, I'm stunned by the nonsense that stumbles out of my mouth.

"You want DVD. Yes, *The Honeymooners*. That will help you relax. Just put the dog down, go to the set and press the play button on the DVD machine."

Petey's man wriggled his legs around the dog, leaving Petey snoring on the sofa, unwilling to waste consciousness on something that had nothing to do with food or a bathroom break. The man padded over to the set.

"Such a good man," I murmured. "Such a responsible, alert man. Now touch the DVD button, and you can watch the funniest comedy to come along since they invented laughter. Only the slightest twitch of your finger, that's all it takes. Such a good, good man."

Yes, sir, I was proving myself to be a born people whisperer. A natural. Grand-slam home run my first time at bat with a sunshiner.

Petey's man bent in front of the set. An index finger jutted out and wove in front of the screen while the man squinted to read the markings on the controls.

"And, a genius, too," I encouraged. "You only need five minutes to find the button with the glowing red light. Such a genius."

My personal nominee for the first Nobel Prize in Machinery Operations hit the power switch and turned off the television.

CHAPTER

"That's a good specter. What a wonderful specter. Climbing into that coffee pot all by hisself. Wasn't he cute? I bet he can climb right out of it now. Yes, he can. All by his little lonesome. Although a couple maps and a GPS locator might help."

The voice was feminine, the tone edgy, the accent Gothic.

I peeked out of the spout of the old coffee pot on the wall where I spent my second consecutive day's sleep, wafted by more aromas than I really needed.

Gilda clapped her hands. "Oh, look at those itty bitty sleepy-time eyes. Poor li'l spook. It must be tough telling breathers what to do. All of that time and energy trying to move them around. Where do you find the energy?"

I squirted out of the coffee pot to confront her. Might as well get the drama out of the way first thing in the evening.

"What's the big deal?" I tried a little theatrics myself, reaching for the sky like a priest placating a really pissed-off deity. "Aren't you the one who brought me here? Knowing these people have DVDs of *The Honeymooners* lying around like banana skins in the monkey's cage at the zoo."

"Excuse me for expecting a little gratitude from a recovery-mate," she said.

"I thought you weren't speaking to me," I said. "The moment a beagle came into my life, you split."

"I wouldn't dream of coming between two mongrels. And I certainly wouldn't expect a spook of your lofty transcendence to notice a lowly recovering spook like me."

I gave her my best glare. "And what 12-step program says ridicule is a good recovery tool?"

"I believe they're called Idiots Anonymous," she said. "But you would know more about them than I do."

And she was gone in a *poof*.

Time comes in the life of every specter when becoming a Tosser looks like a rewarding way to spend your nights. First, you can throw things when you get irritated. Second, you don't have a bunch of spooks in your home-group who feel entitled – obligated, in fact – to critique everything you say and do. Third, you can throw things. Fourth, you don't have to feel like the lowest species of worm if you set a bad example for newbies. And, fifth, you can throw things. Anything you want, really hard, at anyone you want.

I could hear silverware rattling in the kitchen, and cupboards opening and closing. Like a Tosser gathering his ammunition for a truly memorable night.

I drifted through the wall and materialized just inside the last layer of paint. The view wasn't the greatest, but I could see Petey's mother collecting dishes, glasses, silverware and napkins on a kitchen counter. She was motherly in a young-ish way: her brown hair tucked behind her ears, her jeans and man's style shirt chosen for comfort not appeal, her feet clad in the first pair of genuine sneakers – not jogging shoes – I've seen in a month of midnights.

With the ease of a waitress in an all-night diner, she put everything into a stack and carried it into the dining room.

Petey sat at full attention, still unsure if the welcome mat would be rolled up and she'd be put on the road again. Her tail went wagging from side to side as she scampered to me.

We were beginning to establish our routine. I squatted and molded my hands around that furry figure – careful, though, not to let my fingers actually sink into her skin – and gave her a vigorous psychic rub.

"I've got to apologize," I told Petey. "It must be confusing when you're just a dog and somebody expects you to operate a DVD player. There are electricians who can't do that. Although, I wouldn't insult a beagle by suggesting a mere tradesman is in your league."

Petey seemed to appreciate the apology.

The woman set the table, returned to the kitchen and soon we heard the banging of pots and the beep of a microwave. With a warm glance acknowledging our friendship, Petey hurried off to the kitchen. If the chances of getting a scrap of food were one in a million, a beagle would think the odds were too good to ignore.

First stop this evening was Hollywood Cemetery to try my newly acquired skills as a ghost-whisperer. If I couldn't stop Fergus, the least I could do was bring some comfort to the spooks he trapped inside the Squires family mausoleum. I rematerialized beside the bronze door and saw the lock still in place and heard the murmur of a tomb-full of vexatious specters inside.

I imagined being trapped in my coffee pot at home with Fast Eddie and Rosetta. It was enough to take the fun out of being dead.

Once I started talking, the mumble of voices became a maelstrom of shrieks. In the calming, reasonable, assuring tone I'd heard Cal use last night, I tried to gentle their mood, reminding them that they were children of a benevolent universe, that the spiritual principles of our 12-step program were tools for all situations, that it's always brightest before the twilight.

Inside the mausoleum, they weren't buying any of it.

They howled, they screamed, they cursed the sun and the planets. And I knew if, by some chance, one of them could manage to escape through a crack in that sealed fortress, the first order of business would be to find out how much damage one spirit could do to another.

The tomb-squatter who'd helped Cal and me last night was just arriving at his grave across the road. He waved his bat.

"I miss anything?" he called.

"No," I answered. "Got here a few minutes ago myself."

"I hung around until the last possible moment last night – my bedroom is in the eaves of the caretaker's hut down the road. All was quiet."

"The one with the tattoos who brought those spooks to the mausoleum, has he been around?"

The spook across the road gripped his bat. "If I ever see him again, he'll wish I hadn't."

I drifted in his direction. *Henderson* was the family name on the headstone. The Henderson spook was giving the gravesite a careful inspection that pilots checking their planes before take-off could learn something from.

"Let us know if anything happens," I said.

Bending over the base of the headstone, Henderson wiggled the bat over his head in acknowledgement.

It was such a nice twilight that I decided to take a stroll through Hollywood. Not that I had any interest whatsoever in checking the engravings for anyone named *Ralph*. That barely crossed my mind, and then, only to remind me that it would be disrespectful to the dearly departed to ignore their names. I can be quite a stickler for protocol when the spirit – so to speak – moves me.

Despite the chill, it promised to be a pleasant night. A scent of barbecue smoke from nearby homes glided through the air, with just a hint of berries squashed in the road by car tires.

Jedediah rose from the environs of his gravesite as I approached. From a distance in the growing dimness, I could tell the old boy was agitated.

"I hope the ruckus at the mausoleum hasn't been bothering you," I said.

"I think I'm being called," he said, simply.

I stared at the old boy. Not even Cal knew what happens after we leave here, but the consensus was that something highly unusual marks the transition from here to there, making allowances, of course, for a lack of consensus over exactly where *here* and *there* are.

Most spooks are partial to the notion of a deep voice summoning them from a bright light. The Gen-Xers are beginning to whisper about a giant flash-drive that would descend from the clouds and suck them into a celestial microchip. I've always favored tales of a mysterious replica of Las Vegas appearing in the mists, where Elvis ballads draw you toward an astral copy of the MGM Grand Hotel.

I studied Jedediah. "Are you hearing Elvis?"

"Nope, it's the light."

"Do you see it now?"

He shook his head. "That's the crazy thing. It comes and goes. Like they're not sure about me." Jedediah looked at me with anguish. "You'd think if they're giving a spook the call, they wouldn't be wishy-washy about it. I think they're teasing me. I don't care who they are, I don't like that."

"Something's not right." I surveyed the headstones. "Where'd you see the lights?"

"Yonder," he said, indicating a hill in the center of the cemetery.

"Want to come?"

"When the call comes, I've always said I'll be at my station. Don't want folks in headquarters"– Jedediah gave a covert glance upward –"to think I've been spending my time wandering all over creation."

Tell them to leave you alone until they make up their minds I was about to offer. But the anxiety in his face took the words out of my mouth. Jedediah was scared. Scared of what lies ahead, of what he's supposed to do and say, of what he's not supposed to do or say. But mostly he was scared of not being selected. What if the bright luminous light that descends upon a soul at the end of his stay here is triggered, from time to time, by a clerical error? Man's ideas about heaven are fine and dandy, as far as they go, but perhaps we're expecting too much of ever-after to think it's a glitch-free zone.

And, of course, might the explanation for Jedediah's now-you-see-it-now-you-don't light mean it wasn't coming for him? Perhaps it was for someone who hadn't shown up in the vicinity earlier this evening? Someone who was heading up a darkened hill at this very minute with the haste of a startled snail.

Past the first two rows circling the hill, I went around a shed-sized monument with bas-relief soldiers standing guard at each corner. Trees broke up the orderly ranks of marble and shadows, and I convinced myself that a couple of students grappling in the front seat of a car, bumping against the headlight switch, could account for Jedediah's light.

I zigzagged around a low white marker aged by the seasons and came as close to tripping as a spirit can manage, and when I righted myself, I was aware of a curious disturbance in the night sounds. I paused to listen, found myself baffled, and proceeded slowly toward the crest of the hill, now separated from me by only four or five headstones.

Before I reached those final markers, a blazing light ignited on the far side of the hill, sending white-hot streamers tearing through the limbs overhead. A light so powerful that a breather might have been knocked over by the sheer force of its artificial photons, while a spook like myself would soon find himself transported to another level of existence. Or shredded to nothingness.

This light looked like something I'd seen before. I was more intrigued by something else that manifested itself in the dark recesses of the hill.

It was the sound of a human heart breaking.

Seventeen
CHAPTER

hough protected by the hill and the trees from the light that ravaged the darkness, I was blinded by the reflections from leaves. Simple proximity to so much brightness, too, disoriented my none-too-strong sense of direction.

My eyes whipped through ribbons of shadow and streamers of light waving around me, searching for the source of the weeping that began about the time the light came on.

Most memories of the daylight world are hidden to me, yet at that moment I had the conviction that I'd never heard a person cry with such hopelessness.

The light went off, just as Jedediah had described, and the following blackness was stark and frightful. Gone were the details of my world. I was left with the rough outlines of trees and tombs, a general sense of the wind, an approximation of the scent of pine needles. If the ever-after was nothingness, this was the sort of foyer I'd expect before stepping into the abyss.

Because I could think of no reason to head in any other direction, I followed the sound of the crying.

She was a white bundle on the downslope of a grandfatherly oak, shaking and sniffling, so choked with grief that sometimes there were great gasps as she remembered to breathe.

Instinctively, I reached for her shoulder. Before I could touch the gauzy fabric, Margie's glistening face looked up. "Why did I ever listen to you? How could I possibly be so stupid?"

"You want stupid?" I replied. "Take a good look at me. I've personally set the bar pretty high for stupid."

Her teeth clenched. I saw her fighting to force words through her lips. "What kind of an idiot would give me advice on acting? You've done this before, Mister? You know what it's like to stand in front of a camera and bare your soul?"

"I don't know much about anything."

"And even less than nothing about the spirit world. *Help Hollywood see what death is really like* you said. Basement meetings, 12-step programs, recovery. *Get beyond the clichés.*"

"What happened?"

"The director decided to help me get beyond the idea of having an acting career. After laughing his head off when I told him your ideas."

I did a double-take. "You talked to him? He heard what you said and spoke to you?"

"Heard me? I might as well have been a cricket in the weeds for all the attention I got."

"We need to talk."

"Why? For what earthly reason? The last time I listened to you, I got fired."

"It's not what you think."

"Not what I think! What's ambiguous about the words *You're fired?* You don't understand those two simple words? Then I can't imagine why I should listen to you explain anything."

She was right. I had tried to nudge Margie closer to accepting her own demise, and had only succeeded in driving her deeper into her delusions of still interacting with the physical world and further from Specters Anonymous and acceptance of her own post-mortality.

When logic and reason don't work, Hank likes to say, *try brute force.*

I looked at her. "I hope you'll forgive me some night for what I'm about to do."

She fixed a look on me that would have a breather rushing to protect his jugulars. I grabbed her shoulder and went *poof*, taking her with me.

Though I'm not an advocate of force, Hank says a lot of problems in the afterlife can be helped by the *Beam-me-up-Scotty* mode of conflict resolution.

It works like this: Get Margie to a safe place and surround her with spooks in recovery who will talk about their own road to transcendence until Margie breaks through her denial. Informed consent isn't important for this approach, nor is even a rough awareness of what's going on. It's officially called *an intersection*. Hank calls it *a traffic accident*.

Only problem was: When I materialized beside our regular booth at the River City Diner, Margie wasn't with me.

Hank, Gilda and a couple teenagers were spread across the benches. Gilda practically had her head in a girl's lap to smell the breather's waffles and coffee. Hank watched her with an interest rare for someone who had the reputation for being the coolest spook this side of Forest Lawn. An intuition whispered that Hank might have designs on Gilda, and I wasn't at all sure what I thought about that.

Hank barely registered my arrival. "Yo, Ralph. Somebody pissing on your grave? You look ready to run screaming into the sunshine the first chance you get."

"I was bringing a newbie to an intersection," I said. "She was with me and then she wasn't."

"Sounds to me like you don't know the difference between a breather and a spook."

I laughed along with Hank because I couldn't think of a better explanation. Breathers aren't really in our dimension, so *Beam-me-up-Scotty* doesn't work with them. A seasoned specter can shrug off involuntary transportation. But a newbie? They're stuck to you like chewing gum to a shoe.

Gilda bestirred herself from the food. She knew exactly what was on my mind: "Remember what I told you. Our little Margie started hanging around the afterlife before they invented darkness."

"What are my chances of going back to getting the silent treatment from you?" I asked her.

Gilda, wisely, chose not to hear the question. "It's almost enough," she said, "to put me off maple syrup to think what Margie's actual carcass must smell like."

"There's something terribly wrong with Margie, and it ain't her perfume," I said. "She thinks she's alive."

"Maybe she is."

It's not as if the living and the post-living have their own color-coded name-tags: *Hi, I'm Barbie and I'm a Sunshiner* or *My name is Brad and I do everything in the dark*. But we know, we spooks just know.

Gilda's barb struck target. I tried to shake it off. "I've seen a dozen people walk right past her when she's talking."

"That's called good taste," Gilda snipped.

Another dart, sunk deep into my ectoplasm. I slumped and stared blankly at her.

Hank slapped his hand on his thigh. "Don't stop now, children. This discussion is showing the potential to be really memorable."

"I don't want to fight," I muttered.

There was nothing I wanted to say and nowhere I wanted to go. And I was wearied by the triple whammy of having a Tosser and a tomb full of specters I couldn't help, the miserable advice I'd given Margie that drove her further from recovery and, not that this should affect me at all, the light that appeared in the cemetery and might be coming for me.

I barely noticed Gilda push her finger into the bare mid-riff of her benchmate. The woman shivered, told her boyfriend it was too cold to eat and asked if they could go someplace else.

Gilda glided off the bench when the girl started leaving, but Hank made the teenaged stud on his side of the booth slide through him to the exit. The kid gasped as though he just dove into ice water when he came in contact with Hank's ectoplasm.

Hank grabbed my wrist and pulled me into the booth after the sunshiners left.

"I sense our noble spook has an issue of genuine substance interfering with his transcendence."

Gilda lost little of her edge. "Speak, spook."

"It's really nothing," I said. And then proceeded to tell them all about the light in the cemetery that might have been for me, or perhaps for Jedediah, or maybe even for both of us. How can we be sure the light always strikes its target on the nose? Or that we don't get warnings when it's coming for us?

"Shouldn't that be good news to a dyed-in-the-wool 12-stepper like you?" Hank asked.

"But why now? What am I doing so differently that I should be called now? It's not like I've accomplished anything."

Gilda doodled her finger around the abandoned waffles and hoped, I could tell, that this time just a molecule of syrup would stick to her finger long enough to taste it.

"So," she concluded. "Transcendence isn't enough for you. You also insist on understanding it."

"Isn't that the way it's supposed to work?"

"That's the way *this* works." She flicked her other hand in a way that took in the diner, Shockoe Bottom, Richmond, North America, and everything else. "But we're in the bleachers for the sunshine world. We're not really in the game there."

"*When all else fails, quit doing the things that fail*," Hank said, with a good impression of Cal's voice as he intoned one of the master's nuggets of wisdom.

"So where does that leave me?" If I reached for the sugar shaker, I was afraid I'd be able to grasp its ribbed, molded plastic shape. "I put on my best suit of armor, mount my trusty charger and, with my faithful squire at my side, ride out to fix whatever wrongs I come across in two worlds."

Hank nodded. "In a nutshell, yeah."

Things done, things undone. Paths taken or not taken. Armor and vulnerability. My mind was a blender of images.

Gilda stared at me. "What are you thinking?"

"I seem to have misplaced Sancho Panza."

"Huh?" Hank said.

"My squire," I said. "My faithful squire."

Eighteen
CHAPTER

ven with the burst of inspiration about where I'd first heard the name *Squires*, I might have sat in the booth in the diner until the bats came home, watching Hank watch Gilda who was watching me, if I hadn't noticed the waitress tidying up the tables and booths. She scooped a newspaper from a chair, rolled it into a tube and tucked it under an arm, then assembled plates, cups and silverware into a stack to carry to the kitchen.

Faster than you could say *poof*, I was gliding through the foyer of the *Richmond Times-Dispatch*.

Blogs, internets and computers may be the informational wave of the future, but we spooks are committed to newsprint. Partially, we're showing off: we don't have to worry anymore about getting ink on our hands. Mostly, though, it's a matter of access.

If I wanted to waste some time, I could always zip inside any computer and wander around the mother-board. I could kick the CPU, take a ride on the hard drive, and watch the pixels on the screen change color. I could even burrow into a memory chip and see little bitty switches go this way and that.

But what does that tell me? Squat — that's what.

But newspapers and libraries are filled with words on paper. And paper is a medium you don't have to be a medium to use.

Unfortunately, every spook figures that out during his first couple of nights on this side.

"Excuse me. Pardon. Please watch that elbow."

An astral battle-axe made her way through the specters milling about the newspaper's foyer. They were packed in there, wall to wall, and several layers on the vertical. A platoon of rebel infantry lined up against the reception desk. Women in flouncy blouses and long skirts swirled around hip-hoppers with their cargo pants and décolletage racing each other to their knees.

Everyone was fired up with the hope that they were about to find information that would explain their first lives and give them some idea of what they're supposed to do in post-mortality.

"Why are we here?"

Gilda had materialized at my side. I'm not sure whether I preferred her new, I'm-concerned-about-you-but-I-won't-say-anything-because-I'm-afraid-you'll-snap look to the frosted shoulder I've been getting from her lately. I was hot on a scent and didn't have time to figure her out.

"Do you remember when Fergus came to our meeting?" I asked.

"I remember both minutes he was there," she replied.

"He asked us a question. Do you remember it?"

"He was looking for somebody."

"Do you remember the name?"

"Stop jerking my chain, Ralph. You remember and you're about to tell me."

"It was Squires. Tommy Squires."

She looked at me as though she were incapable of connecting that name to the name carved on the mausoleum that Fergus had been stuffing with spooks. Which, of course, was exactly the case. Gilda hadn't been with me in the cemetery, nor had I told her that part of last night's adventure.

While a spectral high school band and a first-life girls' field hockey team clattered through the entrance hall, I filled her in.

After the grand finale (mine, not the band's) Gilda shook her head. "You don't have anything. We knew, fifteen seconds after Fergus showed up at our meeting, that he was looking for a spook named Squires. Now, you're telling me Fergus has found him. So what?"

"So, why trick spooks to go into a tomb they'll never get out of?" I asked. "Why go to that repo house where we followed him?"

"Second answer – because that's where his bucket is. First answer – because he wants to make sure his buddy Tommy Squires is really inside there."

"Does that make sense?" I asked.

She shrugged. "Of course not."

I threaded my way through the crowd to the reception desk. As I guessed, a laminated card lay there with names and telephone numbers for various offices. And with office numbers.

"Follow me," I told her.

Past the newsroom, where dozens of reporters sat, some with telephones pressed to their ears, others scowling at computer screens and a few chatting with colleagues, we drifted until we came to a door marked *Library*.

A small number of employees (Dare I call them a skeleton staff?) were working the night-shift. If they could have seen the herd of spooks crammed into every alcove, shelf and wastepaper basket, they would have come up with a less catchy job-title.

A line of specters formed at the wooden catalogue files in the library, with spooks oozing into and out of the drawers in a steady stream. Less order prevailed at shelves holding bound newspapers, while absolute bedlam was underway in a motorized array that stored clippings in something resembling a gigantic Ferris wheel.

One of the librarians, a middle-aged man generously endowed with a mustache that covered not only his lips but also his lower jaw and the top of his neck, looked up from his computer screen.

"Obit pages for tomorrow just cleared," he said. "I'll print them out so we can start indexing."

He spoke, he thought, for the benefit of three other colleagues on the late-shift, but his words flashed through the spectral assembly like an electric shock. I've never seen a larger concentration of spooks in a small space. Half of post-humous Richmond could have been gathered around the office printer while it thumped out the paper's daily record of deaths.

"One of these days, I'm going to figure out where that breeze comes from," the librarian said.

He patted warmth into his upper arm while waiting for the pages to print and managed to swat several dozen specters, who retaliated by rubbing their lifeless ectoplasmic noses deeper into his bare arms.

Gilda nudged me toward the catalogue files and whispered, "You better move fast." I saw the line was gone and dove into the file drawer marked *Ren-Sti*.

On the chance you might find yourself someday as a near-microscopic, extra-dimensional entity searching through a file catalogue, allow me to offer some advice. First, if you should find Gilda darting between the cards with you, either go home at that point or accept that you'll be following her orders for the rest of your excursion. You'll stay dead longer if you don't fight her.

Second, cruise through the cards in the upper left-hand corner. That will put your arrival at each card in the approximate location of the start of the decedent's last name. Third, much as you may be inclined to scan each card for references to the name *Ralph* – and I can personally vouch for what a fascinating pastime it can be – fight the temptation.

Fourth and finally, if you find the card you're looking for and Gilda is already there, leave right then. Your chances of reading the card within the duration of a normal afterlife aren't worth computing.

After bumping and tussling and grappling, Gilda hauled me out when she was done.

"Now," she said, back on the library floor, "that was helpful."

The line outside the catalogue files had reformed, but I squirted back into the cards. According to my first perusal of the cards, *helpful* was likely to have Gilda fined by the Guild of Posthumous Goths for unseemly optimism.

How does one read the print on a catalogue card when one has squished oneself into such compactness that a loose nose-hair looks intimating? This spook reads very, very slowly.

When I reemerged, Gilda was gone. I drifted down the hallway and ended up floating near the ceiling of the Style section, drawn to the room by the smell of a fresh cup of coffee, which sat on the desk of a single editor manning *(girling?)* her station. I welcomed the chance to get my thoughts in order before Gilda rearranged everything.

Tommy Squires, it turned out, had been a rising star in the local racing circuit, destined to make a name at a national level. But a freak accident with a baby buggy, empty except for a keg of beer and propelled by three college freshman made reckless by the prospect of a dehydrating frat house, sent poor Tommy to that pit-stop in the sky. The only other oddity in the report, in case the immediate circumstances of the death were too pedestrian for a reader, was the remarkable coincidence of the death, two days later, of Tommy's beloved aunt, Alma Allan, who passed away in a nursing home while her house was being burgled. No suspects apprehended.

Gilda was back before the editor could take her first sip of coffee.

"Our favorite repo was where Tommy's aunt lived," Gilda said.

"How do you know that?"

"I did some diving in the phone book. How many Alma Allan's can one city have?"

A repossessed house is a genuine terror of the afterlife. And if you think you're getting *the call* already, it's hard to find an incentive to put yourself through it again.

"You're not getting the call," Gilda said before I could open my mouth.

"Says who?"

"*The Richmond Times-Dispatch*, that's who."

She pointed at today's newspaper spread to the Style section on the editor's desk.

LA's Hollywood Comes to VA's Hollywood
Late Night Filming in Famed Cemetery

If anything, the little house by the river had gathered more gloom since our last visit a couple of nights ago. Thicker shadows hung from the low bushes and dripped from the eaves. On the sidewalk, I felt a chill come from the fractured windows and broken side-boards. I'd guess nobody had lived in the house for years. My own question is how anyone could possibly find out that this wreck had been broken into.

"What makes us sure the house will behave itself tonight?" I asked, sounding totally nonchalant and devil-may-care if it weren't for the deep gulp I needed mid-sentence.

Gilda was tightening the buckles and straps on her all-black ensemble. "We'll be on the look-out for flying elephants."

"And that'll do it?"

"Based on previous experience, absolutely." She looked directly into my eyes, her mouth tightened, her eyes squinted and her voice was barely a whisper when she said, "We're a team, right?"

"'Natch."

This time, the knob on the front door turned while we were climbing the steps, the door swung open, and a strange sound, somewhere between a gurgle and a burp, greeted us.

"Basement or attic?" I asked. "Anything hidden has got to be one of those places."

"Jeez," Gilda said, "I was going to check the drawers in the kitchen first. That's where I used to hide my extra house key."

I was going to ask if she was serious about the kitchen drawers, thought better of it, and led the way inside. If I was going to be subjected to molecular decomposition anyway, why worsen the situation with a bad attitude?

Gilda already had an attitude. She set her heels down with extra force on the floor and triggered a symphony of creaks, cracks, squeaks and groans.

I put a finger to my lips. "Shhh. We don't know how long we're going to be here. No sense alerting the house this early."

Gilda rested her hands on her black leather hips. "But we want the house to know we're here. How else is it going to tell us where to look if it doesn't know we're here?"

"You think the house is going to tell us that?"

"Ducky, it's not going to be able *not* to tell us. I ask you: Does this house look bright to you?"

I knew I was contributing to my own confusion, but I was too distracted to worry about what she was going to say next. So, squinting in the dark, I answered, "No."

And she said, "There you go."

If I were anywhere except in a repo, I would have sat down and refused to cooperate with her on anything ever again. But Gilda walked into the foyer, where dust and miscellaneous debris – shredded papers, twigs, empty tin cans – had gathered along the floorboards like drifted snow.

And silence. You know the kind of silence that's quiet because everything that can be said has already been spoken, all actions have been completed, all dreams fulfilled – that kind of silence?

Well, the repo's silence was the opposite of that.

CHAPTER

Nineteen

We followed a hallway that ran to a set of stairs and, beyond, to rooms whose windows had been boarded over. Gilda charged ahead, and I was right behind her. When she stopped, I stopped, and short of a skeletal claw poking through the ratty wallpaper for my throat, I wasn't going to say a word. Not a peep. And certainly not a whine.

She listened to the house. But my ears still reverberated with the sounds of those poor spooks in the Squires family mausoleum, bumping together, stepping on each other's toes, condemned to wander in a few feet of darkness with specters every bit as frightened as they were.

Gilda reached for my hand. "Do you hear that?"

Before I could sort my thoughts from my memories, the side of the hallway exploded. The darkness had wings, and they beat against my head and neck, fluttered down my collar, scratched my hands. *Cheep, cheep, cheep, cheep.* Not voices from a tomb, now, but from fluttering blackness that rushed past us in a torrent. I turned against the flood, crouched and found clutched in my hands a squirming creature with a fiercely beating heart. A bat! I let it go with a yelp, and I'm not sure if that sound came from me or the flying rat.

"That way," Gilda said, calmly untangling one of the creatures from her hair.

She pointed to the side of the hall — actually a darkened doorway — through which the bats had come.

I hate to admit it — and I certainly didn't intend to make any such admission to Gilda — but I was beginning to see the logic in her strategy. Go in the direction the house doesn't want us to go.

"Do you think it's possible," I asked, "for us to fall through the floor and break our necks in the basement?"

"One way to find out."

Turning from the main hallway into the darker, narrower, bat-less corridor, I noticed the air was colder. For the first time in the afterlife, my astral limbs shivered. An odd sensation rose through the floorboards, as though the house were breathing.

"I see what you mean," I whispered to Gilda's silhouette. "The house didn't want us to come down this corridor, and that's the reason for the bats."

After a long pause, Gilda said, "It could have been worse."

"Such as?"

"Such as: Do you feel something funny around your feet and ankles?"

I was barely shuffling along, trying to hear Gilda above the thunder of her hobnail boots on the hardwood floor. Now that she mentioned it, however, I'd been sensing a mild resistance when I slid each foot forward. As though I was moving through shallow water. Or better yet, across a field packed tightly with cotton balls that resisted every step with subtle obstinacy.

Cotton balls. That was precisely the thing.

A furry squirming bundle pushed against my socks and ended up riding far enough up my trousers to tweak my ectoplasmic skin with a touch reminiscent of dandelions and bunnies.

I giggled and bent down to swat away the sensation.

"I don't suppose this hallway could be packed, five or six inches deep, with cotton balls," I said.

Gilda scraped a boot along the floor-boards, and I heard whisking and whooshing sounds down there. "If there were any cotton balls down there, they were eaten a long time ago by the rats."

"Rats!" In an instant, I understood what was happening. I also understood what would happen if I unleashed my inner coward for a howling retreat: that is, there would be dozens of trampled, mutilated rat carcasses and a cascade of razor-teethed brethren scrambling down the corridor to avenge their buddies.

"Let's keep moving," Gilda said.

"Wouldn't think of doing anything else," I answered. "Can you tell where the rats are coming from?"

"Up there." A rickety staircase emerged from the gloom, with crumpled steps, a broken balustrade and the stench of wood that had passed rottenness and was closing in on liquefaction.

We paused when the last of the rats was gone. The steps led upward to a solid wall.

"This house is playing tricks with us," I said. "There's nothing up there. We could go up there, only to find ourselves stepping into an abyss. Or have the stairs grow teeth and develop a taste for ghost flesh. Or"— I shuddered before the words had even left my mouth —"walking into someone else's tomb, and never being able to walk out."

"Good point," Gilda said. "Maybe you should lead the way from here."

That's the age-old dilemma for deep thinkers. Just because we have a keen-eyed understanding of a problem, some idiot decides we also must have the go-get-it to find a solution. But with Gilda having led the way this far into the repo house, I couldn't exactly call her chicken for giving me the chance to take the point.

"Well, let's get this over with," I said.

Stepping onto the first stairs, I expected a creak. I got a groan loud enough to startle the mumblers in the Squires family tomb.

"Don't bad things happen in threes?" I asked.

"That's just a fairy tale," she said, standing there on the floor as I mounted a decayed stairway to nowhere.

"That puts my mind at ease," I answered.

As I went up, I steadied myself with a hand on the railing. It gave a little shake, as though welcoming me, then collapsed over the side.

"I'm glad that's out of the way," I said over my shoulder.

"Lucky you," she agreed.

Keeping as close to the wall as possible, my shoulder brushed a trail along the disintegrating wallpaper. The stairs were steady, in a wobbly sort of way. A dozen tiny crackling explosions came with each step. I could imagine plaster, wallpaper, leaves and twigs, even fragments of shingles and tiles crunching underfoot.

Below me, Gilda cleared her throat. "Do you have any special aversion to cockroaches?"

"Nothing special. Why?"

"Just wondering." Her voice turned suspiciously cheerful. "Say, do you have a better view of the top of the stairs? Does that really end in a wall?"

I craned my neck. Somewhere a crack in the roof admitted a sliver of light, which happened to fall upon the end of the stairs.

"Yep, looks pretty solid."

"I wouldn't take my eyes off it, if I were you," she said. "You know how things can change here without warning. I'd hate for a door to swing open and a truck to come down the stairs."

I chuckled. "For a skeptic, you spend a lot of time worrying about things that come in threes."

"Sure," she said. "Ah-huh."

About the time I hit the crunchy step at the mid-way point, my shoulder brushed something on the wall that wiggled, and only years of developing my mental toughness kept me from hopping over the side of the stairs. That and naturally slow reflexes.

Whatever it was, it wiggled back into the spot it had recently occupied on the wall. I stared at the dark blot on the wall – well, not really a blot, actually, more like a neatly formed square of blackness – and dared it to try wiggling again. Because if it did, I'd make it very sorry.

"What?" Gilda called. "What's going on up there?"

"I'll let you know as soon as I figure it out."

My unflinching eye was enough to subdue it.

Three or four more steps, and another odd protrusion fidgeted on the wall after a bump from my shoulder. It swung back and forth like the world's most poorly designed pendulum. Just another lump rocking in the darkness, a square lump.

I was beginning to detect a pattern. I was on high alert, and when, after taking another four steps, I saw another rectangular patch on the tattered wallpaper, I flicked it with a finger. It swung along the wall for a few inches, then swung back.

The wall at the end of the stairs was now two steps away, close enough to touch. Sometimes there's a concealed latch, I told myself, or maybe a hidden door that opens with a push. Wherever my finger touched, the wallpaper and plaster disintegrated into a cloud of dust, leaving shallow, rough furrows in the surface.

"That's two theories that bite the dust," I called down to Gilda.

"What?"

"The idea of bad things coming in threes. And the idea that the bad things were trying to keep us from coming here."

"Is there anything up there? I mean, out of the ordinary, anything strange?"

"Only a staircase that leads to nowhere. That's pretty peculiar."

She snapped her fingers. "That's it. The house was trying to keep us away from the staircase, not the wall at the end of the staircase. You're smarter than you look."

"Well, I have my moments," I whispered, trying to figure out what to do from here. As staircases go, this one was nearly gone. Railing on the floor, steps liable to expire at any moment, decades of fallen debris covering the stairs with a grotesque, rustling snow.

I scraped my foot along the step and watched a dark cloud billow upward. I could almost swear some of the litter was moving when it hit the darkness. Walls and floors and pipes and wires that decided they didn't like me were becoming parts my afterlife. But plaster flakes that ran away?

Squatting, I ran a finger along the top of a step. Bits of plaster scurried away. I grabbed a flake and was surprised to find rows of bitty plaster legs on both sides and a little plaster head and little plaster jaws working back and forth. I held it up to the chute of faint light. It reminded me of a cockroach.

"Gilda, speaking of peculiar things, have you noticed anything odd coming down the steps?"

"Odd? Odd? Let me think a moment."

"Something in the area of insects."

"Oh, the cockroaches." Her voice was cheerier than a dead woman who'd been standing in a flood of rampaging insects had a right to be. "When I was a breather, I lived in student housing. I guess I learned not to see cockroaches as any-thing out of the ordinary. They were practically members of the university family."

"Ah, that explains it."

But it still didn't explain what was so unusual about the staircase that the house would try to scare us away from it. The only thing here, except for its pending collapse and the cockroaches (who were leaving anyway) was the odd swingy things on the walls. I went down a step or two.

The light was fainter, but leaning close enough to the wall to practically brush it with my nose, I could make out the barest suggestion of forms and shapes on the surface of that thin, square something that swung along the wall.

Well, no afterlife lasts forever. I shut my eyes, gripped the edges of the mystery object and pulled it from the wall.

I've wondered what it would be like to sit on the edge of a volcano as an ocean of glowing hot lava spews into the sky, or squat in the waving prairie grasses when a tornado goes swirling overhead. I searched for those possible first-life memories as I clutched the object to my chest and waited for the house to respond.

"Have you died again up there?" Gilda called.

"Not yet."

I darted down the steps, crushing generations of cockroaches as I went, and grabbed the two other objects off the walls.

Twenty

CHAPTER

W hen you believe an entire two-story collection of timber, bricks, tar paper, glass, tile, wallpaper, nails, screws, insulation and animosity will topple on your head, getting out of the house quickly is the only thing that matters.

I was fearlessly focused on the mechanics of moving my feet across the floor until I saw the front door in approximately the same location where Gilda and I had left it and realized that the odds looked good for the two of us to leave Alma Allan's with all the ectoplasm we originally brought inside. Then I got frightened.

Okay, I'll admit it I might be overstating the case. But for a few seconds I probably used the planet's entire allotment of fear. During that brief period, lambs lay down with lions, birds snuggled in the fur of cats, and subway commuters showered good-natured greetings upon panhandlers. Then the usual slaughter began again. And I was out the door, onto the porch and flying toward the grass without any thought as to what happens when spooks leave repos.

Let me fill that gap in your education, using myself as a case history. The spook exits the dimension of materiality and reenters the dimension where his sorry little butt belongs.

If I had anticipated this normal return of the abnormal, I might have paused on the porch to examine the three objects clutched to my chest while I was still able to hold them.

As it was, the instant my feet lost contact with the porch, the laws of the afterlife stepped from the weeds and insisted upon asserting themselves. My hands slipped through those objects – old wooden picture frames, as it turned out – which tumbled to the tall grass around the house.

I wanted to put at least the Rocky Mountains between me and this wretched excuse for human habitation, but I glanced at the picture frames that the house was so determined to keep me from seeing. A familiar face stared at me from one of them. I skidded to a halt and made my way back across the lawn.

Sure enough, it was my old buddy and nemesis, Edgar Allan Poe.

Here, in a frame that could have been made with a wood chisel, he looked at the world from a drawing on a yellowing page clipped from an old magazine. In masterful strokes still quite clear, a pen had inscribed beside the drawing:

> *To my beloved cousin, Hiram Allan*
>   *– E. A. Poe*
> *Author of "Tamerlane and Other Poems"*

"I wonder what it means?" Gilda asked.

"It means that Tommy Squires, whose good buddy Fergus has been filling the family tomb with specters, is a distant relative of Edgar Allen Poe."

Gilda pointed to another frame lying at an angle against a clump of weeds and said, "And that?"

Its glass broken, the second frame was empty, except for the ancient backing now visible from the front. Handwriting not as elegant as Poe's was visible along the left-hand side:

> *Edgar Allan Poe*
> *Unpublished poem*
> *Circa 1822*

"Do you see any broken glass?" I asked Gilda.

"Nope."

It'd been a long time since I worked a jigsaw puzzle, but I felt the flush of satisfaction as pieces fell into place. "Look there. The backing's discolored. Something – and a small piece of paper would be perfect – sat there for decades." I sighed. "Just think. That must be really worth something."

Gilda gave me this look. "Naw, just a couple bucks at any second-hand store."

"I'm not talking about the frame."

She whipped up a double-helping of *the look*. "What then?"

"A poem. An unpublished poem by Edgar Allan Poe."

"Why'd anybody care about an old poem?"

"Well, first you'd have to know something about literature. Then you'd have to know something about feelings."

If Gilda could have turned red, I think that's the moment I brought her closest to breaking out into a neon rainbow. But Goths pride themselves on their indifference, and I'm sure she was embarrassed by her unseemly display of emotion. She went *poof.*

The longer I thought about it – an unpublished poem by Edgar Allan Poe, one of the country's earliest and greatest poets and practically the inventor of ghost stories – the more I appreciated the enormity and the value of such a discovery. The old boy might have died penniless and alone on the road, but the public's fascination with the man who wrote *The Raven* is still going strong.

Ghost stories. I'd never really thought of the implications of that before. Might he have had some special insight into the afterlife? Odd, too, that I'd never heard of Poe wandering into the St. Sears meeting or another get-together of Specters Anonymous. I'd expect him to be more interested in all things spectral than the average spook. Wouldn't he want to know if he guessed right about the Other Side in his spookiest tales? Or might he have been so familiar with us during his days as a breather that, once here, he was bored to tears?

Fortunately for me, I don't have to waste time guessing about anything involving transcendence. That's why my 12-step program has sponsors.

Faster than you can say, *Warp speed*, I was standing next to Cal at the steps of the Tobacco Factory, one of Richmond's finest eateries, located in a rebuilt storage barn for the original *devil's weed* on a six-block stretch of shops near the river. The area had cobblestone streets and an ambience that favored midnight strolls, when the city was hushed and footsteps echoed against the brick walls. A touch of fog rolling off the river is always nice.

Much as Cal railed against the newbies who lingered around the shopping malls and other *stumblie places* that remind them of their first lives, Cal favored this section of Richmond when he wanted to clear his mind, especially before meetings.

Cal, you see, had been a brick mason before becoming eligible for Specters Anonymous, and he liked to come to this area to study the ways other men have used brick and stone to construct buildings, streets and sidewalks. Not that it tempts him to return to a daylight schedule: He once told me studying this stretch of the city was, for him, much like an afternoon in a library must have been for me during my sunshiner days.

Before I could say a word, he floated into the street and squatted down to examine the rough cobblestone surface. A cab bounced by with passengers for one of the nearby hotels, and it went through Cal with no more effort than a summer's breeze through a silk scarf. I don't know if I ever would want to reach the point where a taxi shooting through me was no big deal.

Cal must have noticed me squirm, for I got an *explain-thyself* glance. I decided to take the discussion into another, safer direction.

"Why do cars still use this cobblestone street?" I asked. "Do that many people miss carnival rides that have them bumping up and down on their seats."

"You think this is a bad street?" he asked, his eyes never leaving the cobblestone.

The thing about sponsors is that every question is a trick question, except for the ones that aren't.

Slowly I answered, "I think it's pretty. The way the round stones poke up here and dip down there. Very, um, artistic."

"Yes. But is it a good road?"

It's tough being part of a metaphor-in-progress. It's even tougher when you know the lesson that's lurking around the corner is one that could dominate your night, perhaps your week, and this might be the decisive moment to help shape it. There is, however, the impediment of not having the slightest idea what is going on.

"Yeah," Cal said before I could unclog my thoughts. "It has the same effect on me. Do we say it's a crappy piece of construction because breathers are banging themselves senseless whenever they drive here? Or do we say the men who built it must have been geniuses because it's still here after all those years."

"You took the words right out of my mouth, Cal."

He straightened up, dusted his hands through force of habit and, after returning to the sidewalk and shoving his hands into the pockets of his trousers, started heading toward Shockoe Bottom.

I told him about the adventure Gilda and I had had at the repossessed house and, although his disapproval at two spooks new in their transcendence taking on such a risky assignment was clear, he let me get to the end of the story before commenting.

"So, you think the long-lost poem by Edgar Allan Poe is in that mausoleum?"

"Fergus found out about it. And, he decided he'd get one of our spooks to read it to him. Then he'll pass it along to a friend who's still a breather."

"Very interesting," Cal said. He studied me with a keenness I associate with being measured for a suit. "It brings me to something I want to ask you."

"Yes?"

"What have you done this wonderful evening to help a poor, still-suffering specter?"

"So much has happened since I got up. It's been one thing after another. Where does the time go?"

Cal nodded toward the river and said, "There. I understand you might find a newbie or two at this time of night. And don't be late for the meeting."

Don't you just love a strong assertive spook?

The James was running high for this time of year. Thirty or forty feet above the middle of the river, I saw spooks drifting against the current. There were two or three dozen of them, all bunched together so closely they might have been holding hands.

"Ahoy," one of them called across the water.

"Ahoy yourself," I answered.

"Would this be Providence town?"

"What?"

"Our ship was homeported in Providence. The good ship *Bessie Anne*, she struck a rock in the Dardanelles. Can you direct us home?"

About the only thing I truly hate about after-living near the water are the crews that pass on an endless journey through the skies.

When I had my bucket on the island, I tried a couple of times to explain to the ghosts of sailors why they didn't want to go home: if they really found their homes or even a memorial that marked their passing, their chances of moving on to real transcendence plummets. And now, once again, someone's asking for my help to reach that fateful, fatal destination. From sheer laziness, I favor honesty. But, what's kind about a truth that consigns them to a non-existence like Henderson's or Jedediah's, waiting alone at a gravesite?

A glimmer caught my attention. Margie stood on the river bank, glowing in the moonless night, her face a mask of concentration.

"You're going the wrong way," I shouted to the wind-borne crew. "Go down river, east, until you reach the ocean." I glanced at Margie. "Then turn right. Rhode Island is to the south. That way."

With a smart salute, the captain thanked me and started bellowing orders to turn his crew around.

"I see I got your usual treatment," Margie said. "It must give you deep satisfaction to hurt so many people."

"I don't hurt people. But former people, spirits, entities whose material lives are behind them – I sometimes have to bruise their feelings to get them to recognize where they really are. Who they are now."

"You're very good at it. You must be so proud."

She spun around and disappeared into the shadows. Her words smarted, but not enough to deter me. This was her moment of truth. She would either begin working on her own transcendence or continue to waste her afterlife.

You can't force a dead man to stop breathing, Cal always said.

But, like I'm starting to say, *To hell with Cal.*

I darted into the darkness, calling, "Margie. Just a couple minutes more. It's important. Please."

Edgar Allan Poe sat on a rock on the river bank. I practically oozed through him.

"Did a spook just go by here?"

"I see living people," Edgar Allan said.

"Good for you. But Margie? Did you see her?"

"They're everywhere."

"Yeah, yeah, yeah. She was wearing white, and she had a kind of glow."

"They're walking around like regular spooks. But they don't see each other. They only see what they want to see."

I looked into his haunted eyes. "What are you trying to tell me?"

"They don't even know they're alive."

Twenty One

CHAPTER

or a dead poet, Edgar Allan Poe had a mean dive. Before I could ask him about a poem given to his cousin Hiram Allan a long time ago, Edgar A- honored me with a display of his prowess on a diving board.

Knee-length black coat flapping like a bat's wings, pasty hands cupped over his tousled black hair, he plunged toward the river. About three feet from the waves, he veered upward, hesitated, then dissolved into the night. But I'll hand him something else: death hasn't silenced him. He's the only spook I know who can express exactly how eerie it is at times for us specters to move through the world of breathers.

I'd gotten myself cross-ways with Richmond's adopted poet laureate early in my decedence. Once when his name came up during a 12-step meeting as an example of the efforts sunshiners put into digging their own graves – dead at forty of drink and drugs – I protested that he wouldn't qualify as a true substance abuser, not by modern standards.

Edgar Allan Poe could get drunk on a single glass of wine, I informed the meeting with the authority that comes from having read a single article on the subject, and the drugs he dabbled with were stuff that many people of his time used to moderation and eventually set aside without drama.

The great ghost got wind of my critique and ever since has not missed an opportunity to give me a tweak, especially when I was on the verge of doing something that would add luster to my reputation as a recovering breather.

Through the streets of Richmond I drifted for a while, wondering where I'd be if I were Fergus and where Fergus would expect me to be, so I could be somewhere else. I even joined a party of Confederate dead floating in formation above Hamilton Street until I got tired of the geezers pointing at one co-ed after another and asking me if that's what a "woman of fallen virtue" looked like today.

About a half-minute before the St. Sears meeting was scheduled to begin, I sailed down the street and landed at the top of the steps leading to the basement door. Gilda was staring at the grass.

"Look," I said, "if I ever develop a potty mouth, it'd be a step up in the after-world for me. I'm sorry for sounding like a jerk when we were talking about that poem by Edgar A-."

"Then why did you say it?" she said.

Because I'm a jerk was the easy answer. *Because my mouth is hitting the speed of light while my brain is still under the sheets* was another. I looked at her. In the darkness by the wall, she was barely a shadow. Her head was lowered, she couldn't look me in the eye, her face was a glowing mask.

"Because," I said, "sometimes you remind me of me."

I slipped through the door, nodded to Cal and Fast Eddie and Hank, and took my place above a gray metal chair. For several minutes I sat there with my hands clenched between my knees, unable to hear any of the discussions rattling around me. Sometimes you have to crawl into a private place to get your bearings.

Eventually, Rosetta's voice pierced my bleakness. "Oh dear. I had asked one of our newest members to lead tonight's gathering. It's so refreshing to hear a personal story that's still pink. But, perhaps since our leader was unable to join us, I might ask if someone else —"

The door flew open and crashed against the wall. Darkness settled on the portal. Rosetta gasped. Hank rose to a fighting stance. Cal glanced up with amazing animation, which is to say, an eyebrow moved.

I was afraid to look up. Gilda was entitled to balance some scales, and this wasn't going to be pretty.

But it wasn't Gilda who stepped inside. But Margie. Glowering.

"Ah," Rosetta said, clasping her hands. "Here's our leader now. Everybody, please welcome Margie."

The protocol at 12-step meetings is that the leader takes a seat and stares at the floor for fifteen seconds before saying anything. It's a way to remind the group what spooks would look like if they wouldn't kill to have a captive audience.

Margie stayed by the door and swept the group with a glare.

"When I first came here – or whenever I've bumped into one of you on the street – you've always been so kind. *You gotta start taking care of yourself*, you tell me. *You gotta admit that you're powerless over sunshine. Gotta face the facts.* Well, I'm here to say that you have to start facing some facts."

Darleen blanched, which is quite a trick for a specter. Fast Eddie snuggled down and waited for the entertainment to begin. Hank gave her a serious once-over, seeing as how he liked spooks with a spark. Cal, having expressed everything he wanted to express with his previous twitch, did nothing.

"You're a bunch of losers," Margie wailed. "Losers! You can't go five minutes without getting together to discuss what you should do next. How do you people manage to a buy a bottle of shampoo without taking a vote?"

With a sickly smile, Rosetta motioned to an empty chair. "Why don't you take a seat, dear, and make yourself comfortable?"

"I am comfortable." Margie stepped far enough into the room to kick a chair. "I was born comfortable. I don't need you to tell me how to be comfortable."

I stared at the chair's thin gray legs and watched them vibrate. Shampoo? Vibrating chairs? I was beginning to get a bad feeling here. When I glanced at Cal, he could have been sleeping with his eyes open.

Cal barely moved his lips. "Then why are you here?"

"To tell you to quit making me uncomfortable." Margie was screaming now. "I can take care of myself. Thank you, very much. I don't need your meetings, I don't need your clichés, and most especially, I don't need you telling me how to live my life."

"Life? What life? What's she talking about?" Darleen was confused.

Margie didn't hear her. Nor notice the fidgeting from the rest of the group. Her eyes bored into me like a hand-drill going through jelly.

"And you! How dare you tell me that nonsense about the afterlife. I told the director and it cost me my job. That was my big chance. And you made me blow it."

The door on the other side of the room opened as I was trying to assemble the bits and pieces of a defense. A black face peered inside.

"Are you alright, missy?"

"Fine," Margie said. "Just fine. Thank you."

The breather nodded. The door started to close. Then it opened again, and he glanced over the room.

"Was someone in here with you? If you don't mind my asking. You were talking to someone."

"Nobody. Absolutely nobody."

Again, the door closed. I heard the bolt click with a metallic whisper.

When I looked back at the other door, Margie was gone.

I locked my eyes on Cal. "But she . . . I mean, could . . . Was that what I —"

"*Yes* to everything," Cal said. "We call a breather like her a *two-fer*."

The rest of the meeting veered between discussions of anger management and demonstrations of its lack. Cal had the last word, which was usually the case for him, even if he was the first to speak.

"A two-fer isn't any more responsible for being a two-fer than we are for being spooks. Most of them aren't even aware they're different from other breathers. What counts is how they handle their mortality. And what they do with their awareness of our side of the Great Divide."

"If I were her, I wouldn't have any interest in us," Rosetta said. "It's not decent."

A somber mood pervaded the room even after the meeting ended, and no one seemed inclined to linger for the usual post-discussion discussion. Sadness drifted through our basement hide-away, almost as if a friend had gotten the call or one of us had announced he'd had enough recovery and planned to spend tomorrow at the beach.

I didn't want to talk about 12 steps or listen to anyone else talk about them. But I didn't want to be alone. I headed out to the island to see if anyone had rebuilt the old shack. Halfway there, I realized the island had more emptiness than I could deal with at the moment. I redirected my ectoplasmic feet to the diner in Shockoe Bottom.

Most of the spooks from the meeting were already there. Instead of scattering in booths where they could share the food-smells of the breathers, they had gathered at a table in the back. I floated into an empty seat. Gilda watched me with hooded raccoon's eyes.

"Well, that was certainly an entertaining moment," Fast Eddie said. Looking at Cal and Rosetta, he asked, "Did you know Margie was a two-fer?"

Both shook their heads. Rosetta said, "Gracious, no. One has suspicions, but you're never totally sure. Perhaps in retrospect, I can see that I'd missed signs – the way she kept her feet on the ground. But then, most newbies do that anyway."

"Cal?" I asked.

My sponsor shook his head. In a rare flash of common sense, I decided not to push it.

"Poor kid," Hank said. "She's got to be wondering what side is up."

Darleen, who managed the rare trick of being a spook who hyperventilated whenever controversy was in the air, looked ready to snap his head off, but I couldn't tell whether it was because Hank wanted to give Margie a bad time or because she thought he wanted to help Margie.

"How about you?" Gilda asked me. "Do you think we were a little rough on poor little Margie?"

I nodded.

Cal looked up. "Did I ever bring up the notion of helping another poor spook in recovery?"

"But Margie is a breather."

"I tend to see her as a future spook," he said. "Do what you can. We owe her that much for messing with her head."

Gilda looked steadily at me and whispered, "Yes, you do."

All the astral currents were functioning normally. Within seconds after leaving the diner, I was drifting over Marshall Street as Margie clattered through the darkness below. I was willing to have another go at explaining things to her, I really was, but she looked so small and the sidewalk was so lonely, and I was afraid of scaring her, regardless how carefully I made my appearance.

She seemed brave in a heart-breaking way. Brave for being a tiny woman on a dark night. Brave for being jobless and without friends or anyone who'll worry if she gets home late. When she disappeared under the foliage of an elm, I got nervous and darted ahead. But Margie kept coming, her high heels sounding on the pavement like hammers at a construction site.

She turned into an unlit two-story brick building in Jackson Ward. Hovering in the night outside, I followed her progress through the house as lights came on in the foyer, then a stairwell, then a small window on the second floor squeezed between two larger darkened windows on either side.

I've been called many names in spookhood, some downright inventive, most rather common but straight-forward, but *Peeping Ralph* hasn't been one of them. Why I drifted close to that single window when the light came on, I can't say.

Perhaps to get a feel for what her life is really like. Maybe because I didn't want to return to Cal and explain why I had nothing to show for my efforts. Again.

Margie sat on a bed. The furnishings were austere, standard fare for small apartments catering to students. The TV was off, the radio silent. She sat like a prized pupil waiting for her favorite teacher, back straight, head erect, hands clasped in her lap. Then, as she slowly raised her hands, she also lowered her head. I could hear her sobbing through the closed window.

I don't have a clear recollection of getting back to the townhouse by the river where I'd spent the last couple of days. Full awareness didn't return until I was gazing at the coffee pot on the thin shelf near the ceiling. I looked at the neat dining room table, its polished wood glowing warmly, the *Honeymooners* DVD glistening like a diamond on the table next to the television, and some sort of little plastic men – transformers, I think, or characters from an action movie – lying on the living room rug, while a brown attaché case sat on the table by the front door.

I drifted into the foyer and up the stairs. All the doors on the second floor were open. A middle room on the left betrayed a glowing night-light. I went inside.

The beagle, Petey, raised her head from the bed where she snuggled with James William, the sleeping boy's arm stretched across her shoulders. To me, then back to the boy, then back to me, the dog glanced. If I called her or waved, I was sure Petey would jump from the bed and scurry into the hall to greet me.

Dog and boy – they had a right to their comforts. I glided out of the room and down the stairs.

Twenty Two
CHAPTER

Whoever coined the phrase *dead to the world* had insight into the spiritual dimensions. After I climbed into the hobo coffee pot I was using as my bucket, nothing short of being poured onto the lawn at high noon could get my attention until sundown.

On this day, however, I was roused several hours before twilight by an insistent hammering. I noted the moment and rolled over in my bucket. I heard Petey jump on the sofa and growl at the picture window. Seconds later, the beagle was whining; her claws clicked on the hardwood dining room floor as she ran under the serving table below my coffee pot.

Although I drifted back to sleep, where the image of Margie slumped over and crying awaited me, I have a dim recollection of rising toward wakefulness a couple more times. With the fourth volley of raps, Petey was in the foyer by the front door, snarling for all she was worth. The cool press of early evening slipped into my ersatz sleeping chamber.

"Go away," Gilda yelled from the hallway. "You've got the wrong house. Besides, no one's here."

My first thought was that only Gilda could be unable to get along with a dog that goes through life with a smile and a frisky wag of the tail for everyone she meets. My first image was of Gilda's last somber look at me last night and the steel in her gaze when she nodded her approval to Cal's plan to have me help Margie.

So, let's put Gilda down as one more member of the Boy-Am-I-Disappointed-in-Ralph Club.

I spurted from the spout and found myself in the foyer behind Gilda and Petey. Both were staring at the closed front door.

"Is Fergus out there?" I asked.

"Worse," Gilda replied.

Petey looked up with an expression that told me she was working on her grammar and hoped to communicate with me soon; I saw only one way to get a better understanding of the situation. I thrust my head through the door.

Standing on the stoop, having a bad-hair day and wearing a white gown that had troubles of its own, was Margie. She was more surprised than me.

"What are you doing here?" she asked.

"What about you? Are you following me?"

"If I had even the tiniest suspicion of the slightest idea that you'd be here, I certainly wouldn't be here." Margie stared at me. "But why are you here?"

"This is where I sleep."

The answer took her aback. "Oh." She sidled to the wrought-iron rail around the stoop and leaned against it. "Oh." If I thought modern women were capable of swooning, I'd have rushed to support her.

"My turn," I insisted. "What brings you here?"

"I had this . . . this . . . um . . ."

"Intuition?"

"Actually, it was more like an itch. Not that I think you have any right to know about my itches. Or that I'm the sort of woman who would discuss them with the likes of you. Although you look just like the kind of man who would insist on hearing about them."

I was beginning to get a feel for the way Margie's gears meshed and said, "You were telling me about your intuition."

"Of course I was." She took a deep breath. "I couldn't sleep a wink last night. I was so sure a glorious acting career was right around the corner, and now I don't know where I'm going to get five dollars for a hamburger and coke. *But whenever one door closes, another opens*, my granny always said."

I could feel Petey lying on the floor and trying to press against my ankles, which were now on the other side of the door. For an uncommunicative woman, Margie sure talked a lot.

"I see," I said.

"Then I was walking down the street, and I saw this door, and I knew — I just absolutely, positively *knew* — that this was the door that would open for me. I knocked, nothing happened. I went away, and walked the longest time. But then I found myself walking past the same door again. I knocked again. I must have come back here seven or eight times —"

"Four. You were here four times."

"Of course it was four. Don't confuse me." She paused, and I wondered if I really cared to find out how this would end.

"So, I'm here because this is the door of opportunity that's going to open for me." She gave me a slit-eyed glance. "Well? Aren't you going to open it?"

"Actually, I don't do doors," I said. "And there's nobody here who does. When I say nobody, I don't include the dog, who's here and technically capable of opening a door, except that she isn't."

"Good gracious," Gilda stepped through the door and knocked me aside. "She's got you talking now like she does."

Gilda looked levelly at Margie. "You want a door that will lead you to hamburgers and soft drinks?"

"Oh, yes."

"Follow me."

Gilda led us downtown, along streets and side-streets I didn't recognize. When I say *led*, I mean that she and Margie walked side by side, their shoulders brushing each other's, while I trailed behind.

"I like what you've done with your hair," Gilda told Margie.

Margie ran her fingers though a hair-do that would normally be proof of electrocution. "Oh, this old thing, it's nothing. I must say I wish I were so bold to wear chains and black leather. Outside the privacy of my bedroom, that is."

"A spook does what a spook has to do."

"Yes, indeedee." They both giggled. Margie leaned over and, confidentially, asked, "Do you like being dead?"

Gilda patted her arm. "I haven't broken a nail since the funeral."

"Oh, goody."

I groaned.

A few blocks ahead I made out a traffic light and the side of a bank building on Broad Street. A quick right, another left, then through an alley and out to another street. Gilda stopped beside a tired brownstone house, where a too-familiar bay window with a neon sign proclaimed, in winking letters: *Psychic Advisor*.

"Of course, why didn't I think of this?" Margie said. "They can look into a crystal ball or read some cards or study my hands and tell me which door to open. This will be fun. I've always wanted to see a real side-kick. I mean, someone outside of the movies."

"It's pronounced *psychic*, not *side-kick*," Gilda said. "And instead of going to see one, how about becoming one?" Gilda looked at me, and for the first time in my after-(or first-)life, I actually saw a lump go down a someone's throat as she swallowed her pride. "Wouldn't that be fun?"

"And people would pay me?"

"That's the idea." Gilda smiled weakly. "Let's see what the job entails, shall we?"

I've got to hand it to Gilda: she certainly hasn't let death interfere with her salesmanship.

"After you," I said, although, being incorporeal, I couldn't do the gentlemanly thing and open the door.

Margie stepped onto the stoop; the door flew open. Two women on the well-maintained edge of middle-age came out, followed by a spook I remembered from my early nights in Specters Anonymous.

The one with the jawline that Mother Nature had nothing to do with, was shaking her head until her dangling pearl earrings actually swooshed through the air.

"Was this Bunny's idea of a joke?" she asked her companion. "I'd always wondered if she and Alfred had a . . . well . . . interest in each other. But to feed me that swill about the amazing Madame Sophie. About how that fraud could help Alfred communicate with me. That was going too far. That woman will never do bridge in this city again."

Alfred — for that was the spook's name — gave me a guilty wince. "If you'd have seen Bunny in her prime, you wouldn't hold it against me."

"A dead romantic," Gilda huffed. "Who would have guessed?"

The woman's companion was fussing through an industrial-sized purse for car keys. I could imagine them getting into a car and driving into a permanent parking space in my conscience. Along with Margie, the two-fer, whose unemployment I'd contributed to.

I roused those jaundiced little cells in my head from a long nap and said, "Alfred, isn't there something you want to tell your wife? Something very important?"

"Yeah, I want her to know I'm sorry. And that I got it out of my system."

"Ah, can you come up with something more personal?"

"Sure." His smile was quickly eclipsed. "Like what?"

"Like, what did you do for fun in your first life?"

Alfred got a twinkle in his eye.

"Forget Bunny," I insisted. "Tell me something you talked to your wife about. Your private way of relaxing."

"There was golf. I got a hole-in-one a few years back. And I might have had my best score ever on my last game if my putter hadn't crapped out on the ninth hole."

I looked at Margie. "Tell her that right now. Before they get away."

"But we haven't been introduced," Margie said.

"I'm sorry." Alfred's widow looked up. "Did you say something?"

"Go ahead," I pressed. "Do it now."

Margie looked like a twelve-year-old as she said, "I'm sorry to bother you. But Alfred said he's sorry about Bunny. That he got her hole once. And that he was having his best game when his – I don't know how to say this to you – his *thingee* gave out."

"His *thingee*?" the widow asked.

Margie looked expectantly at Alfred, then at me. I thought Margie was doing a better job of getting the woman's attention than anything I could have thought of.

I threw up my hands. "Why not? His *thingee*."

"He says: His *thingee*. On his ninth try," Margie told the pair.

The other woman stepped between Margie and her friend. "Who? Who's saying this."

I was reaching my night's limit for chaos. I pointed to Alfred. So did Gilda.

So Margie pointed at Alfred and said, "Him."

The widow grabbed her arm. "Can you see him? Is he here now?"

Margie nodded to Alfred, who was drifting between Gilda and me, which, of course, would appear to the breathers as an empty space, which, come to think of it, wasn't that different from actually seeing Alfred.

"Tell me what he looks like?"

"He doesn't have much hair, at least not on the top of his head. His eyebrows are nice and bushy, though. And I've heard a lot of women really like men with bellies."

"Oh, Alfred." The widow collapsed into her friend's arms.

"You can take it from here," I told Margie, not letting it become a question.

"You betcha."

"And you," I said, moving nose to nose with Alfred, "you hang around a while and help my friend Margie."

Alfred yawned and backed away. "Thank you, very much. This has been a lot of fun. But I've had enough excitement for one night. I think I'll turn in early."

"If you leave now, don't expect my help when Bunny crosses over."

"Bunny? Coming here?"

"People are just dying to get in.

Twenty Three
CHAPTER

ilda and I took a stroll by the river. The air became richer, mellower, and I wanted to fill my lungs with the smell of decaying moss and wet sand. But specters can only sniff, and for the moment, that was enough.

I glanced at Gilda. She seemed to enjoy testing the old routines – if only in play. Putting her feet down on the earth and moving forward by rotating forward on her ankles and pushing off.

"What did you think about that? Back there?" I asked.

"You mean, why did I help Margie?"

(Note to self: Quit trying to sneak up on, sneak around, or sneak anything past a spook of the female persuasion who makes fashion statements with metal chains.)

"Yes. Why?"

Gilda surrendered to the question. For once. "I wanted her to go away. The only way that would happen was for her to get what she wanted."

"A lot of spooks wouldn't have handled it like that."

"So, a lot of spooks are jerks."

Not the sort of remark I like to hear while taking a walk in the cool of the evening along the river with a spook who, despite the studs in her black leather gear, sometimes had this intriguing sparkle in her eye.

Margie had now met a woman who might be willing to pay for the sort of information about the Great Divide that Margie knew without trying. If Madame Sophie was the best this city had to offer, it wouldn't be long before Margie was the top side-kick advisor on the East Coast.

"You have your own little surprises." Gilda said, stooping to pick up a rock to toss into the river, then straightening before her fingers could sink through the tarry surface. We all forget from time to time what *normal* looks like.

"About Bunny," she continued. "I didn't know you could tell when a breather is going to join us."

On a usual night, I would have gone into my aw-shucks-ma'am-'tweren't-nothing-special routine. But even nights in the afterlife can have a little magic in the air.

"Don't let Cal know you caught me in a fib."

She smiled.

I don't believe either of us said anything more. The river burbled in the dark like a contented infant. On the opposite shore, the lights from distant Petersburg softened into a faint haze. Not until the walkway curved and we emerged from behind tall buildings that blocked the inland neighborhoods from view were we able to see blue and red lights flashing near the water in the distance.

Not terribly far away. About where the townhouse where we'd been staying was.

Poof, poof. Gilda and I disappeared in a wordless staccato and instantly rematerialized in the street in front of our home. Pulsing blue and red lights were joined by the steady glare of auto headlights, giving the street a fun-house aura. The kind of fun-house where visitors never laugh and all the residents cackle.

The door of the townhouse was open to the flashing lights that probed the dark interior. Clustered in the tiny lawn near the steps were the boy James William, his parents and the dog Petey.

I sniffed the air. "Where are the firetrucks? There are enough cops here to open a donut store, but where are the firemen?"

"Off fighting fires," Gilda whispered. "That's not what's happening here."

"Then what? A burglary? An assault?"

Gilda glanced at the ground. The street was covered with rocks, carpeted with them, buried inches deep in places by stones and pebbles, as were the sidewalks, the small patches of grass that passed for lawns, and the hoods and roofs of cars parked on the curb.

Slowly, my eyes began to register the scene. Most of the windows in our townhouse were broken, and in some, I could trace the trajectory of fractured glass and, several inches below, the punctured cloth of curtains.

My fault, my fault. The words ran through my mind like a sick mantra. *My fault.*

Fergus the Tosser wasn't going to play fair once he figured out I was interested in his afterlife. I should have faced the facts long ago. But would he know that I'd already identified the mystery treasure as a poem by Edgar Allan Poe? Would there be some advantage, some edge, in playing dumb and leading him on?

But on to where? Another downside to letting yourself stop breathing is that a proper dust-up with a peer is complicated. How are you going to hurt someone who's already dead?

"I've got to make sure Fergus isn't here," I said. "That's about the only thing I can do now to help."

At the front steps, the family — my family — was pressed together like newborn puppies in a box, eager to touch, rub against, nudge each other. I heard the *clickety-clickety* of Petey's toenails as the dog scurried up the steps behind me. The *Beam-me-up-Scotty* mode of astral travel could have me hovering next to Fergus in a billionth of a second. In two billionths of a second, Fergus could be discovering exactly how much damage one spook could inflict on another.

In the foyer, with lights from the police cruisers shooting through the door like water from a fire hose, I glanced down to thank Petey for joining me. The beagle's breath hung in gray puffs.

This was a house on the way to repossession.

Bats and rats and cockroaches had guided me to the spot that the repo house on Laurel Street didn't want me to go. Here, I had Petey. After fortifying my courage with a glance, the dog headed inside to the stairs and scampered to the second floor, with me following.

From the upstairs hallway, a low growl crept along the carpet from the door that opened to James William's bedroom.

"Good girl," I told the beagle. "You stay here."

But Petey kept marching forward. The look she gave me from the doorway could launch a revival of the blues on this side of the Great Divide. Then, lowering her tail and ducking her head, the dog entered the bedroom.

Stealthfully, I approached and, just outside the door, I reached out to steady myself on the wall. Another one of those habits that sticks around longer than the lilies in a funeral home.

I expected the wall to be solid to my touch, like any other repo or, if it was mostly in the physical dimension, my hand would slip easily through it. But this house wasn't a full repo. Not yet, at any rate. When my hand touched the surface, I had real physical contact with something from the material world.

From the material world, but not totally there. Try imagining walls made of huge, thick rubber bands. Put pressure on them, and they'll flex inward until you lose your balance. And my balance left a long time ago.

Pulling myself upright, I listened intently for clues, then entered the room.

Fergus sat on an enormous pile of rocks, whose base filled the floor. The bed was buried in the rubble, as were chairs, mirrors, little boy's shoes, and little dog's leather bones. That pile was so high that Fergus had to stoop to keep from plunging his head into the ceiling, which he did from time to time anyway.

"Do you know what I want?" he asked.

"Other than peace, clean water, a five-dollar martini and universal brotherhood?"

"No, what I want instead of that crap?"

"You tell me."

Fergus pitched a stone to the floor. It missed Petey by inches.

"No," he said, "you tell me."

I don't waste my nights with two-bit Beelzebubs telling me how to run my afterlife. But when Fergus bounced a softball-sized rock up and down in his hands, I realized Petey wasn't built for quick maneuvers.

"I think you look like a spook with a deep appreciation of American literature," I said.

Fergus studied me for a moment, then, with an air of disappointment, set down the rock.

I patted my leg to get Petey's attention. The dog began to pick her way to me across the rubble.

Stalling for time, I said, "I don't understand what the big deal is. A poem has been sitting in a frame in that house for decades —"

"Closer to two hundred years."

"So why is it suddenly a big deal this week?"

"Because old lady Allan was an idiot. Because my buddy Tommy Squires was an idiot. Because I was an idiot for not moving faster when Tommy told me he was related to this Poe fellow and his great-aunt had some of the guy's scrib-blings." Doubt creased Fergus's forehead. Perhaps for the first time in this or any other life. "I don't know, maybe I moved too fast. If I'd been a little slower, I might have been more careful crossing the street."

"Well, you've learned your lesson," I said, cheerily. "You'll never do that again."

Fergus glared back at me.

(Another note to self: Never try to charm a Tosser.)

I tried a different tack: "Was it a good poem?"

"It had the old coot's handwriting and his signature. That's all that matters."

"So," I began again, "you don't have to worry about it now, do you? You are, after all, dead."

"I told Tommy's sister Ramona I'd get it. And that's what I intend to do. I'm not going to let some legal technicality stop me."

"*Legal technicality?*"

"Brain death."

His voice filled the room like an arctic blast. Petey scurried faster to me, her head down. On the pile of rocks, debris dribbled downward; I felt the floor tremble as though an earthquake was beginning.

I said, "If I get it, will you leave these people alone? On second thought, will you leave them and me and this entire area alone? Better yet, this continent isn't big enough for the two of us. There are volcanic islands that might appreciate having a new deity."

Fergus responded to my suggestions with a scowl, and I decided it'd be rude to waste his time right now finding out what he expected me to do with the poem if I got it for him.

He didn't seem like the type overly concerned with administrative details.

"Get the poem," Fergus said.

"Keep your ectoplasm on."

Fergus grinned. Frost poured from his mouth in a geyser. "You know what breathers say about the road to hell being paved with good intentions."

"I've heard that one."

"In my world, they say the same thing about the insides of mausoleums. I'd enjoy helping you find out if that's true."

Gilda was sitting on the front steps when I emerged from the house with Petey.

"Don't tell me." She raised a hand. "I could hear him from here."

"How's it going with the family?"

"The cops told them there's an epidemic of gang-related vandalism. Probably initiation rites. Would you believe, somebody trashed an old building downtown so bad this week that it has to be demolished."

"Nah! To a historic landmark? Those beasts!"

"That's sort of what I thought," Gilda replied.

Halfway down the walkway, I watched a young man in a trench coat approach Petey's father with a business card in one hand and a narrow notebook in the other. He introduced himself as Brisk Briscow, reporter with the *Times-Dispatch*, and he wanted to know if the family had any idea what happened. Had anyone seen suspicious activity lately?

"Like kids walking around with rocks stuffed in their pockets?" Petey's dad said.

"No," said the reporter. He had a short wiry cut to his blonde hair and a physique far too lean for a reporter. And a tendency to blush, he had that, too.

"I'm thinking," Briscow said, "about kids being where you're not used to seeing them."

"You mean, in school?"

Briscow's blush deepened. "We can continue this discussion tomorrow, sir. After you and your family have had a good night's rest."

For once, Petey's father didn't have a snappy come-back. With a dull gaze, he watched policemen drive stakes into the front lawn and string yellow tape to keep out the curious.

"Good luck, sir," Briscow said, following the older man's eyes. "I understand the police are going to watch your place tonight for safety. I'm sure you can move back in tomorrow."

Petey's father gathered James William, Petey and Petey's mother and ushered them into the family car.

Gilda and I watched them drive off. Then Gilda glided toward the front door, which by now was sealed by police tape.

"What are you doing?" I asked.

"Flaunting authority," she answered.

I was about to remind her that sneaking through a police line was hardly a significant act of rebellion for either of us anymore. But, of course, it wasn't the cops to whom she was thumbing her nose.

Twenty Four
CHAPTER

ergus was gone by the time we got inside, but through an unspoken agreement Gilda and I settled into the living room for the rest of the night. The lights from a fleet of patrol cars outside reflected off the *Honeymooners* DVD on the TV table, reminding me of Christmas in a combat zone. When a crew from the fire department tramped through on a safety inspection, we drifted into other parts of the house. The firemen may be on a different plane of existence, yet it seemed that we were underfoot.

Gilda nodded at the DVD. "It can't be easy for you, being this close to something that might have the answer you're looking for."

"'Natch." I chewed on the thought as a fireman with a barrel chest and hands as delicate as a dancer's thumped over the floor. "Do you ever wonder why you wrote *Gilda* in that book?"

She held out her leather-clad arms. The chains twinkled shyly. "The name's alright. But for the death of me, I don't understand why I need to look like . . . like . . ."

Gilda paused to watch the fireman stomp his way back across the living room, and I sensed that she had strayed into a realm of her first life that she was uncomfortable sharing.

"I think you look very fetching in black leather and chains," I said.

"That's not what they say in the Portlands."

I felt a small truth, not a big one nor even an important one, but a truth that called for respect in its own right, pacing around Gilda in the dark. I had to ask, "What exactly did they say about you?"

Gilda's chest heaved. It couldn't be a sigh. Even if she could manage that trick in the here-after, she was the last spook I'd expect to try it.

Then she said, "They said I was frightening babies and little dogs. That it was my kind who gave ghosts a bad name."

By now, the fog from the river was rolling through the open door of the townhouse. I had never seen a spook cry and somehow seeing Gilda on the verge of tears was as frightening as watching Cal start sobbing.

"None of that matters," I said. "What counts is that we learn whatever we're supposed to learn here. Or solve some puzzle. Or fix some problem. Or do whatever's keeping us from advancing further in our transcendence."

Gilda gave me a look I'm sure I saw in a bar on the face of a guy who asked me if I'd be willing to bet twenty dollars that he couldn't sink an eight-ball in a corner pocket.

"What's the last thing you remember?" she asked. "I mean, right before you stepped out of that processing center and entered the afterlife?"

"There was a turnstile. And a door. And an exit sign over the door."

"What did the sign say?"

I shrugged. "Exit."

Using her index finger like a pencil, Gilda wrote in the fog:

Exit.

"Hmmm?" she asked with a triumphant smile.

This was too strange even for the afterlife. I was beginning to see why the spooks in the Portlands weren't sorry to see Gilda go.

"That's what it said," I said.

"Are you sure?" She waved her hand, sending currents swirling through the fog and before the astral lettering was lost to the night, I saw the letters twitch and hop into the tiniest rearrangement:

Fix it.

As the night deepened and I sank further into a morass about meaning and fairness and atonement, the firemen left, as did most of the cops. A single policeman remained to protect the house from burglars. Perhaps the fellow had some psychic abilities, or maybe he was simply being prudent, but I couldn't help noticing that he never let go of the handle of his billy-club.

"What are you going to do?" Gilda finally asked when the cop finished one of his periodic walk-throughs and returned to the kitchen.

"I'm going to make sure Fergus never frightens any more little kids. Or dogs."

Gilda's eyes gleamed with a dark fire. "You've got your own police force here? Your own courts? For spooks, I mean."

I grunted. "I heard some spooks tried to put together a jury once. Twelve members, sitting in judgment of another spook. They ended up with fifteen different verdicts."

Gilda shook her head and studied the floor. She was beginning to remind me of Cal. Not one for talking, although Cal liked to hang around with other members of the posthumous crowd, while Gilda seemed to force herself to keep from crawling into the shadows by herself.

"Is this a disappointment for you?" I asked, not sure what I meant or expected her to say.

"It's okay," she answered. She had a slight smile. I don't believe she expected that answer herself.

As morning twilight spread across the sky, we drifted into our coffee pots for the day, confident that the clean-up crews would leave us alone. I fell into a restless sleep thinking of Petey, confused and frightened in a motel.

By the time we reemerged in the early evening, most of the townhouse's broken windows had been replaced, and I could smell primer on window sills and frames. James William's room had been cleared of both rubble and furniture, his clothes and toys transferred to cardboard boxes that lined the hallway, his bed and desk on the back lawn. The little room reeked of disinfectant and new paint.

"Well," Gilda told me with a shrug. "This has been surreal. What's the schedule for today?"

"Fix everything."

She bobbed her chin. "Great, I like having a plan. What's the first step?"

"Figure out how to fix everything."

"We're making progress already," she said.

Was that a glimmer of amusement in her eye? I wasn't used to being part of a two-spook team. So far, the only team the afterlife has taught me to work with had a nightly meeting, with endless discussions before and after the meeting.

"Let me think about this for a while," I said, although I'd done all the thinking I intended to do during those lonely daylight hours in the bucket. I didn't want to drag Gilda any further into my feud with a Tosser. "If you have anything to do in the meanwhile —"

"Sure." A shadow of uncertainty made its way across Gilda's face. For the briefest instant I was afraid she would challenge me, say that I didn't trust her, when the one I didn't trust was myself and how I'd react if Fergus did anything to her.

She shook off her doubts and said, "I promised to meet Rosetta at the diner after sundown. Maybe you and I can get together before the regular meeting."

"I'd like that."

Perhaps another spook would have given me a hopeful smile before *poofing* away. But Gilda was a Goth, and she favored me with a momentary glance directly into my eyes that felt better than the warmest hug.

I spent a long time wandering through the townhouse, checking each closet and drawer, although I don't know what I hoped to find. My plans for Fergus were an amorphous haze, almost like a mental thunderstorm, and I came to realize that if I were alone with them much longer they'd hurt me. I thought about heading to the diner but set my astral automatic pilot for the Tobacco Warehouse. Cal was nowhere in sight. Instead of looking for him in his other – pardon the technical language here – haunts, I went back to the cemetery.

Henderson, the tomb-squatter near the Squires family mausoleum, was back at his post. At least, one unending vigil had its amusements. With his baseball bat cocked over his right shoulder, he'd taken a batter's stance facing an elm tree several rows away.

"Hey, want to catch for me?" he asked.

Not having any commitments until the usual meeting, I said, "Sure."

I crouched behind him, punched my hand into an imaginary glove, and dredged up baseball patter from my childhood.

"Come, batter, batter, batter. Come, batter, batter. Hey, batter."

A leaf broke loose from the elm, caught the breeze and drifted towards us.

"Swing, batter, batter, batter. Swing."

Henderson lifted the bat higher over his shoulder; he leaned on his right leg, the muscles in his arms and back, which weren't quite there anymore, tensed.

The leaf floated closer, coming right at us.

"Hey, batter, batter. Can't hit it, can't hit it, can't hit it."

My patter didn't break Henderson's concentration. His eyes never left the drifting speck of yellow-orange, now growing steadily larger. He leaned back on his leg, the tip of the bat traced a tight little circle in the air.

"Go for it, batter. Go, go, GO."

A couple feet from Henderson, the leaf must have hit a cross-current, for it dropped a few inches, rose several more inches, and veered abruptly away.

"Leaf one," I called.

"Pretty good curve on that one," Henderson said. He stepped back and tapped the soles of his shoes with his spectral bat.

"Yeah," I answered. "Some of those elms throw a mean leaf."

Henderson nodded. Where baseball was concerned, he didn't find anything funny, and I saw another needless sorrow in a tomb-squatter's afterlife. A regular spook can always go to the ball park to watch a game in season. Heck, he could step up next to the batter and take a few pitches whenever he wants. Who's to know? But a tomb-squatter is always on duty. I had to admire the tenacity of these spooks.

"Any change with your neighbors?" I asked, nodding toward the Squires mausoleum.

"Naw, it's been pretty quiet this evening," he said. "In fact, I haven't heard a peep out of anybody in there."

"Maybe they've all lost their voices."

He gave me a puzzled look. "Can't say that I've ever heard of that happening to our kind."

"I believe you're right."

I crossed the road to the tomb and, keeping a safe distance from the door, listened. It was as quiet as a tomb.

"Is anybody in there?" I asked.

Pandemonium hit the mausoleum in force. Six or eight voices started jabbering at once, some screaming, others speaking gibberish, a few talking in normal sentences, although it was impossible to make out anything except an occasional word.

"That's so sad," I said. "Once the producers of *Great American Cemetery Choruses* learn that the world-famous spooks of the Squires mausoleum can't carry a tune in a sand pail, they're going to move on. Everyone will be so disappointed and no one will ever visit this tomb again."

"No, they're not."

"What?"

"They're not going to do any such thing. That would be silly."

A single voice came from inside the sepulcher. The rest of the trapped horde was silent. A male voice, it had a slight English accent, tending toward breathy, which is quite a trick for a spook, creating an impression of earnestness and patience.

Against my better judgment, I moved closer to the door. "Why are you doing this now — letting just one of you speak?"

"Because I was just voted spokes-spook."

"Couldn't you have done this a couple days ago?"

"Democracy isn't the easy way, is it?" the voice replied. "There's townhall meetings, flyers to design and distribute, a campaign staff to hire, pollings, interviews, debates. And that's just the primaries. Then there's general election."

"What was the final tally?"

"The official count hasn't been validated. One of the candidates is seeking a recount."

"I'm looking for rough numbers."

"Speaking approximately, the apparent winner received two votes, there was a five-way tie for second with one vote each, and one candidate received no votes."

"What sort of an idiot can't win their own vote?"

"Don't you call my mother an idiot."

"I apologize. Would you wait a minute, please?"

I moved away from the mausoleum. Henderson had taken a classic, well-balanced batter's stance as he waited for the elm to hurl another leaf into the strike zone. Jedediah had risen up from his gravesite to peer over a hill and find out what the commotion at the mausoleum was about. Down the road, a ragged column of rebel soldiers marched across the cemetery, their arms swinging at various tempos, some barefoot, some hatless, each carrying a spectral rifle in a totally unique way, while an officer yelled at them for forgetting to shave.

I looked up at the blank, dark sky and screamed, then returned to the mausoleum and said, "I'm back."

"Why did you go away?"

"Unreality check. I was afraid for a minute I was losing my mind." I tried to seize as much control of the conversation as possible. "Did the reason you got talked into going into the tomb — did it have something to do with a piece of paper?"

"You mean the poem?"

Suddenly, a halo of Oreo cookies whirled over my head. I heard Norman's Smackernackle Choir singing the *Atta-Boy Chorus*. I wanted to throw up my hands and go running down the hill. After, that is, I figured out a way to throttle the spook on the other side of the door.

"Can you read it to me?"

"Yes, I can. The writing is quite legible, what we used to call a good clean hand."

When the spokes-spook stopped, I assumed he was getting the paper with the unknown Poe composition. Seconds dragged into minutes.

"Are you still there?" I finally asked.

"Yes."

"I'm waiting for you to read the poem."

"Oh, I can't do that."

"But you just told me it's legible."

"It's very legible. And I'm not stupid. You're trying to get me to read the poem. Then you'll go away, quite pleased with yourself. And we stay in here, thoroughly miserable until the sun becomes a big lump of burned-out charcoal."

"No, I won't."

Someone began to hum on the other side of the bronze door.

"Really," I persisted.

The humming grew louder and more out of key.

What would Cal do? Besides avoiding getting into a situation like this in the first place. Maybe I could get Hank: He's pretty good when it comes to reducing problems to the simplest solution, although those solutions tend to rely upon brute force, which does have some gaps in the afterlife when measured for credibility.

Having no alternative was no alternative. For I remembered the evil glint in Fergus's eye as he hefted a rock last night and glared at Petey.

A line from our 12-step program's literature fluttered into my frozen mind. To achieve transcendence, we were required to have *tooth-pulling honesty*, maintaining levels of integrity that breathers only approach in the presence of a dentist with pliers in his hand.

"Let me get back to you," I said. "Okay?"

There was an explosion of voices inside the tomb. I thought I heard someone say, "We'll be here," but it was hard to tell.

Across the road, Henderson was tracking the trajectory of a leaf that the wind was carrying toward his gravesite. He leaned back, kept his eyes on the leaf, and when the fluttery piece of orange and yellow was near his outstretched left foot, he swept the bat, level with the ground, in a mighty *swoosh*.

This being spectral baseball, of course, the leaf kept drifting past. I called out, "That's an easy double. Maybe a triple."

Even spooks need to win one from time to time.

Twenty Five

CHAPTER

*L*eaving the cemetery, I had a close brush with a stumblie, for I knew, from the depths of my toenails, that if there were a patch of sunlight anywhere, I'd rush right into it. I wanted to lose myself in the light, to let the brightness pulverize my shadows. If the sunshine couldn't cure anything, it would at least deaden my senses.

I didn't sign up for the afterlife where I'd be responsible for puppies and families and spooks who knew less than I did. I wanted the here-after with quiet walks in the moonlight through golden streets, hours listening to harp music, maybe the chance to ask Evel Knievel what the Roth he was trying to do on that motorcycle.

But, as Cal would say, *Life is like a card game. You only get to play the ace if it's actually in your hand.* Pinning your game strategy upon playing a card you wished you'd been dealt isn't going to be very successful.

I needed a meeting.

My regular get-together with the St. Sears group wouldn't start for more than an hour, but sometimes the newbies show up early. Spending time with a newcomer would be better than listening to Cal tell me how great it was when people really knew about transcendence.

Instead of materializing inside the meeting room, I pulled myself together on the sidewalk outside. Through the window I saw Fast Eddie glide between the gray metal chairs with a swarm of black dots whirling around him. As though Fast Eddie were being attacked by punctuation marks, which, keeping in mind some of the damage he'd done to the language, shouldn't be entirely surprising.

But black dots? I squinted. Not dots, but coffee beans, following him in the air, while he sprinkled them around the room to give the folks in our group the familiar aromas of a sunshiner's 12-step meeting.

"Do you think that's a good idea?"

Cal had materialized beside me. He, too, was watching Fast Eddie.

"He means well," I answered.

"Serial killers mean well." Cal shook his head. "Every time you act like you're a member of the material world, you're one step closer to thinking you can handle sunshine."

"Does that include using a breather to solve a spectral problem?"

Cal scratched his head. "Are you going to hurt the breather?"

"No."

"Transcendence isn't always neat and tidy. If the breather isn't going to be harmed – preferably, if the breather doesn't even know what's going on – I think it might be okay."

Funny how sometimes the trickiest problems can abruptly dissolve like mist on the James.

"I'll catch you after the meeting," I said. "Tell Gilda I'll see her later tonight."

Cal was mouthing the phrase, *Tell Gilda*, with a puzzled expression as I left.

I left the church for sorority row, where I found Hank on his usual patrol to protect the estrogen-carriers of Richmond. I was still assembling the plan in my mind, but knew the pieces that included Henderson and Fast Eddie.

After explaining to Hank the roles for the other two spooks that I needed him to supervise, I knew I'd better deal with his major objection before he had the chance to bring it up.

"Afterwards, we'll all take care of Fergus," I said. "Box him in and confuse him. We give Margie a couple minutes to do her part. Then Fergus can howl at the moon all he wants."

"I was thinking about giving him something special to howl about," Hank replied.

"That's so much like you. Always thinking about your fellow spook."

The next stop was the newspaper. The lobby of the paper was stacked, three high, with spooks socializing, trading notes, waiting for space to open up in the paper's library or trying to leave. I backed out to the sidewalk, rose upward along the side of the building, and entered through the stone wall.

Spooks were shoulder-to-hip throughout the sports section, peering around editors who were assembling the scores from across the country and reporters working the phones for articles about local games or drafting their pieces on computers. The obit desk and the police reporters had a handful of astral noses poked into their business.

I found Brisk Briscow, the reporter who'd covered Fergus's attack on my new home, alone at his desk in the back of the room. He was multi-tasking. For a while, he'd stare at a blank computer screen. Then he'd swivel his chair and stare at a half-dozen pieces of paper that covered his desk, each liberally decorated with doodles, telephone numbers and handwritten notes that could have been made by a dying chicken's last steps.

On one of the slips of paper, I saw *Madame Sophie* written with a line drawn through it and *Crackpot* scrawled beneath.

Three sides of his desk were marked by a low wall that probably rose to his waist. Those mini-walls were covered with cloth, their surfaces were dotted with articles torn from the paper, print-outs, post-it notes, business cards and a few pieces of candy in cellophane – all held in place by thumb-tacks.

Drawn to two envelopes stuck there, I squeezed myself into the thickness of talcum powder, oozed into the envelopes and maneuvered through the folded papers inside until I was ready to emerge with some information about our erstwhile reporter that I could use to fashion a persuasive ring through his nose.

Next stop was a small apartment in Jackson Ward.

Margie was sitting at her dressing table. She had a dish-towel wrapped around her head and a melon on the table. Muttering softly to herself, she waved her hand around the melon, all the while studying herself in the mirror.

Ever since my funeral, I've been snubbed by mirrors, so Margie didn't see me standing behind her. I was there long enough to get the picture. She was practicing for her professional debut as a spiritualist: a little *abracadabra* here, and a touch of *open sesame* there, a proper crystal ball and a generous scoop of hokum, and the kid was going to be ready for the big time.

"Hoooooo," she said. "The spirits are about to speak."

"Perhaps I should come back later," I replied.

Margie spun around, saw me drifting there, peered back over her shoulder at the intruder-less mirror, then turned slowly back to confront me.

"I know you've done a lot to help me," she said. "But I still expect visitors to knock before they come into my home."

I stretched my arm to the wall and made three rapping motions, which, owing to inter-dimensional lack of synchronicity, resulted in my knuckles sinking through the wallpaper.

"That's no excuse," she said.

"I'll do better next time." I floated to a straight-back chair and did my best imspookanation of someone sitting with his legs crossed. "Do you really come from a farm outside the city? Remember, that's what you said at our meeting."

"Sure. I'm surprised I've gotten all the hay out of my hair."

"And the way people on that film-crew treated you like you weren't there? Like you were a ghost? What was that about?"

She blushed. "They were helping me stay in character. I don't think they do that for Meryl Streep."

"Well, Meryl Streep could take lessons from you about being a psychic." I was reaching the limits of my capacity for small talk. "How did things go with the new friend you met at Madame Sophie's last night?"

Margie lifted a clump of twenty-dollar bills. "Would you believe, she gave me all this just for repeating what her husband told me. She said she had friends who'll give me more if I can do the same for them."

"Sounds to me that Hollywood's loss is fortune-telling's gain."

Margie wrinkled her nose. "But I'm not a fortune-teller. I don't see weird pictures in my head. People just talk to me. And some of them happen to be dead."

"That bothers you?"

"The dead people? No, I've been seeing them all my life. I thought everyone did."

"So, what's wrong with getting paid for it?"

She shook her head, and dimples of gold appeared on the walls as the lamp-light caught her hair. "Because I feel like a fraud. I'm not doing anything so special that people should give me money."

I saw her point. "Think of it as being a translator. Lots of people know two languages. No big thing for them. But the folks who only know one language will gladly pay someone for those skills."

"Translator. I like that."

She smiled, I smiled, and I felt a case of dopiness was about to crash on my head.

"Ahem," I ahemed. "You're ready for the next step. Your business needs customers. And to get customers you need –"

"– more dead people."

She looked so hopeful that only with the greatest difficulty could I say: "– you need advertising. And fortunately for you, I know just how to get your name in the papers."

The Squid's Beak Inn was on the dark side of the James, where the fog rolling across Shockoe Bottom could erase an entire city block faster than you can say *Stephen King*.

As Margie and I headed for a booth in the back, we passed three men at the bar. They wore pea coats, watch caps pulled to their ears and a glaze in their eyes that took decades to develop. Smoke curled up from ashtrays, an old jukebox played the same jazz saxophone number continuously. If the place had a bartender, he did a good job of not annoying the clientele.

We had barely settled in when the front door opened with a squeal. The hand on the door knob was attached to a guy who was no stranger to the tougher parts of town: you could tell by the way he swatted away the smoke that rose up and rushed at him.

He saw Margie. She saw him. And suddenly, the three palookas between the guy and the dame weren't enough to register on anybody's radar screen.

Me, I don't worry about radar. I'm a spook. I always fly stealthily.

"Remember not to look at me when I talk to you," I added for the twenty-seventh time. "Don't show him your hand." She thrust her hands under the table. "And don't let him pin you down on specifics."

Margie did a quick canvas of the bar. "Must be my lucky night. I don't see any specifics around that he could pin on me."

"I'm glad to hear that."

The reporter sidled around the three drinkers as though they were china dolls that might break if he brushed them. As he approached us, he was more nervous than anyone in a joint dedicated to senseless intoxication and random violence had a right to be.

"You're Margie?" he asked.

"Yes. And that makes you Mr. Briscow," she said cheerily.

"Brisk. Please call me Brisk."

He slid into the bench on the other side of the booth. He was beginning to look as dazed as the regulars up front, but I'll give the kid credit. He pulled a narrow reporter's notebook from a pocket, uncapped an old-fashioned fountain pen and, tools of his trade duly collected, tried to look at the beautiful, golden-haired girl as though he came here four nights a week with a goddess.

"I must say," he said, "I was prepared to be skeptical when you told me you were a psychic who had something for me that was too important for the phone. I was talking just earlier today to another mind-reader —"

"Madame Sophie."

He straightened, hesitated. "Yes, Madame Sophie. I must admit I thought she was —"

"A crackpot."

Briscow slumped in the booth. From the way he eyed Margie, she could have been a three-headed mermaid regaling him with tales of Ulysses and Marco Polo.

I gave Margie a nudge. As rehearsed, she said, "I guess you're here because I was able to give you an accurate reading of your blood-cholesterol."

"Funny thing, that. I just got a report from my doctor. Hadn't even opened the envelope yet. Just stuck it on my wall."

"Well, your blood is fine. So you won't have to watch your calories when you go to your college reunion." She leaned toward him. "You are going, aren't you? After all, it's just a couple blocks from your office."

"How do you know these things? I just got the invitation."

Much as I didn't care for the melodrama of Margie's rehearsal in front of her dressing room mirror, I thought she was a little too understated now when she replied, "A little birdie told me," and looked straight at me.

"This bird," Briscow said, "is it what they call your *familiar?*"

"He wishes."

"Now see here," I protested.

But Margie went faithfully into the little spiel we'd worked out. Starting with telling Briscow that he'd find some old picture frames on the lawn of Alma Allan's house on Laurel Street. One would have a hand-written note and signature from Edgar Allan Poe. For the other, it wouldn't take a forensic scientist to realize it once held an unpublished poem by Poe.

The reporter looked up from his pad. He'd been writing everything down, in part, I thought, to spare himself the dazzlement of looking at Margie.

"Where is this poem now?" he asked. "Has your birdie passed along any information?"

"In Hollywood cemetery. In a family vault. And the name on the stone is"— Margie cupped a hand next to her ear and bored holes the size of gravel pits into me with her eyes —"the name is . . . . Oh, speak to me, little Tweetie. It's Squires."

Twenty Six
CHAPTER

Reporter Briscow insisted that we stay in the booth for a few minutes after he left. Why anyone in his right mind – or even someone with a mildly homicidal bent – would care about our departure times was beyond me. But it gave Margie a chance to burn off nervous energy.

"I can't believe how easy that was," she told me. "You find out things using your own ghostly methods. You tell that to me. Then I tell them to somebody else. Preferably, someone with money or a job at a newspaper."

"I wouldn't say that's *all* there is. There are complexities, nuances."

Margie wasn't having any complexities or nuances. "Where do we go next? A race track. You can find out which drivers are going to win, then tell me, and I'll bet on them."

I shook my head. "It doesn't work that way. I'm a spook, not a seer. I can't tell you what's going to happen. I only know the things I can see or hear."

"The bank!" She shouted the word loud enough to draw the attention of the goons at the bar, who'd been joined by a fourth. In perfect choreography, the quartet shifted their stools a few inches closer to the back of the room. All sat with a heavy list to starboard, which was the general direction of Margie and me.

"Sssshhhh."

"The bank!" she repeated in a thunderous whisper. "You can be there when it opens. Stand there, all invisible and everything, when they unlock the vault. Only, you're memorizing the combination, then later tomorrow night . . ."

"Tomorrow night, Mr. Briscow will interview you about your role in finding the long-lost poem by Edgar Allan Poe. When the story comes out, your future as a psychic will be assured. My debt to you for losing your job in the movies will be paid. I'll ride off into the sunset."

I didn't add that this scenario still fell short of getting a happy ending, because I'd still be stuck spending the foreseeable eternity in Fergus's neighborhood.

Margie's eyes seemed to glitter, so I added: "I can still visit you from time to time. Would you mind?"

Margie shook her head. "No, I'd like that. But those men at the bar are looking at me like I'm kooksy. They think I'm talking to myself. I don't like people thinking I'm kooksy."

She buried her head in the crook of an arm.

Why do I bother? I can find a nice empty coffin somewhere, climb inside and never have contact with another bruised human ego. But I keep volunteering for this aggravation.

After Margie regained control, we slipped outside without incident, although once we were on the sidewalk, one of the goons from the bar joined us.

My ability to defend Margie was limited. About the worst I could do was to slip through the goon and hope he'd run away when he felt a chill in the air.

It was, as they say, my best shot. I lowered my head and darted for the man's solar plexus. Maybe with a little luck I could give him a bad case of the hiccups.

When I hit the guy, my head was shoved into my shoulders and I bounced backward from the collision. This was no mere stalker. This was a spook.

"You wanna try two-out-of-three?" a familiar voice said. "I wasn't ready just then. Try that when I'm focused."

Hank pulled himself upright.

"Why are you following me?" I asked.

"If I was following you, you'd be the last one to know." Hank brushed imaginary dust off the sleeves of his astral trench coat. "I'm here because I like the atmosphere inside. My kind of place."

"Now that I think about it, I shouldn't be surprised."

"Ralph, perhaps you could introduce me to your friend." Was it a trick of the light or had Margie's eyes doubled in size. She reminded me of Petey staring at her food-dish.

"Hank, this is Margie. Margie, Hank." Margie made a mewing sound, Hank swiped the back of his hand over his mouth and did a bobble-head nod. "Hank is one of our spooks. Remember you're looking at an astral projection. The real Hank is decomposing somewhere with the help of a few thousand ants, rats and worms."

"Lovely to meet you," Margie cooed.

I was about to throw up.

A taxicab pulled to the curb before I had the chance to gauge my chances of finding enough in my stomach to make hurling worthwhile.

The driver rolled down his window. "Give you a lift, miss? This isn't the best part of town for a young lady to be walking alone at this hour."

"Oh, I'm not —" Margie caught herself before she could say *alone,* although I doubt an experienced driver was going to have any trouble reading the meaning behind those wide eyes and the cooing lilt she now gave to each syllable.

"You'd better take the ride," I said. "We'll catch up with you tomorrow."

"By *we*," she said, "I believe you mean *the two of you*."

Hank went bobble-headed again. I said, "Sure. You're going to have to let us know if Briscow can open the tomb."

"Well, then. Later, then."

"Miss? Are you alright?" The cab driver started inching his taxi forward, despite Margie leaning across an open door to smile at Hank.

"I'm just saying goodbye," Margie said.

The driver's worried gaze swept the darkened sidewalk that, to a breather's way of viewing the universe, was populated by a single young woman in an impossibly white gown.

"Who to?"

"Oh," she said, dreamily. "To a tall, sturdy, strapping, powerful . . . oak!"

I never thought *oak* was a four-letter word. In Margie's mouth, it should be banned from decent society. I looked at Hank. He didn't know whether to grin like an idiot or run away or ask her to repeat herself.

Instead, he did what all good spooks do in this sort of situation. He went *poof.*

I didn't begrudge Hank his *poof.* One of the things we learn in the afterlife is the power of a good *poof.* Too much of our first lives was spent balancing on dug-in heels as we proved to ourselves – under the guise of showing the world – that we wouldn't be intimidated.

So, we're not intimidated. We're pummeled instead.

Guess my mind was on fights worth having and fights to walk away from as I left the Squid's Beak Inn. At a breather's pace, I veered inland to pass through Cal's favorite hang-out by the Tobacco Warehouse.

The literature of Specters Anonymous talks about us *taking a bar-code of our actions*, mapping out the sunshine we'd brought into some afterlives, the shadows into others, and the confusion we've spread throughout the here-after and during our first lives.

On the whole, I thought I'd done what I could for Margie. If everything worked out, I'd also be able to boost Edgar Allan Poe's reputation by one poem and help those poor spooks in the Squires family mausoleum.

Fergus bothered me. Forgive me for not feeling sorry for having neglected to bring sweetness into his afterlife. I'd rather strap him to one of the searchlights of Margie's film crew and hit the power button. Which would be a pretty rotten thing to do, even to Fergus.

Not that it would stop me if I had the chance.

Hank flickered into shape on the cobblestones beside me.

"If Cal sees that smile on your face," I said, "he'll have you writing out your bar-code until your arm falls off."

"I'm a spook. I can't hold a pencil."

"Trying explaining that to Cal."

Hank fell into step beside me as we approached Shockoe Slip. A dim light reflected onto the cobblestones from a bookstore wedged between darkened restaurants. To keep the title as the best bookstore on any floodplain in the western hemisphere, folks have to put in the extra hours. I glanced warily at Hank. Some things were none of my business, but I'd never found that to be a good reason to keep my mouth shut.

"I couldn't help noticing you and Margie together," I said. "With you being a spook and her being a sunshiner –."

He waved away the rest of my sentence. "No bother. I don't believe in mixed relationships," he said.

The sidewalks and streets were bare of breathers, the restaurant lights were winking off. A heavy fog rolled off the river, and with visibility limited to a couple of blocks, it was easy to believe we had slipped back a century or two.

"I've been thinking about Fergus," I said. "It's hard to like the guy."

"He's real good at being hard to like. In fact, I'd say that's one of his strengths."

"'Natch," I said. "But we're supposed to help the poor, still-suffering spook, who's having trouble accepting that he's been locked out of every ice-cream parlor in the physical world."

Hank gave me a once-over. "So, Mr. Super-Recovery, exactly how do you propose to touch the heart of a jerk who goes through the astral plane like a wrecking ball?"

Before I could respond – and I intended to remind Hank that our 12-step program requires us to, quoting the literature here, *extend the ghostly hand to all specters in need* – a rock dropped at our feet, hit a cobblestone and caromed into the darkness.

"I don't like being called a jerk."This from Fergus, hidden somewhere in the fog.

Hank glared into the mist. "Hey, Freddy Flintstone, you want to come over here and try that trick with the rocks?"

A dozen rocks zipped through the night, all landed at once and all within inches of us. Fergus laughed. He had a laugh made for a dark, misty night on an empty street.

"He thinks he's going to scare us," Hank said, prodding my arm.

Actually, Fergus didn't have to try hard to tie my spectral shorts into a knot.

"Fergus," I called. "It's all set. Your poem should be freed by this time tomorrow."

"And if you're wrong?"

A couple tons of rocks plummeted into the street to form a six-foot wall directly in front of us, extending as far as I could see in either direction.

"Hey, this isn't necessary," I said.

"No," Fergus answered. "But it's fun."

Twenty Seven
CHAPTER

My return home was unexpectedly complicated. Hank said good-bye with a hasty *poof*, and I was left alone to stare at a wall of rocks that grew a foot taller every ten or fifteen seconds. If Fergus could do that, what could he do to a brother spook who'd gotten under his ectoplasm? What if I dematerialize and, before getting where I'm going, find myself brained by a piece of rock with unknown powers and end up as a collection of molecules floating through the emptiness of space for eternity?

I ended up thinking so much about Fergus's unproven powers that I frightened myself. I wouldn't take the *Beam-me-up-Scotty* way out if my afterlife depended on it.

I tried going around the rocky wall that Fergus dumped on downtown Richmond and must have traveled at a breather's pace for three or four minutes and still had a pile of stones at my side. The only possible explanation, of course, was that I'd lost my bearings in the fog and was going down the middle of the street, not across it.

So I peeled off and headed 90 degrees away from the wall. With a few minutes of trudging, I lost sight of the wall and was still on cobblestone. As though, once again, I'd been heading down the middle of the street.

At one point, I almost stepped through a guy. Through long first life habit, I excused myself, did a quick side-step and kept on going; it took a few seconds to realize the guy was a metal statue. But then, when I turned back to search for him through the thickening waves of fog coming off the James, I couldn't find him.

And folks wonder why spooks run around hollering like idiots.

Fortunately, I was able to find the river bank without falling in, and, keeping the water to my right, managed to make it back to Tobacco Row, then to my townhouse by the water.

Gilda was coming down the inside stairway when I glided through the door. "Hey," she said.

"Hey, back," was my snappy reply. "Anything going on up there?"

"The family's been working all night. They're not going to wake up even if Fergus comes back."

I eyed the collection of boxes and bags in the foyer. There wasn't this much pandemonium when I left earlier in the evening.

Gilda read my mind. "They're moving out."

"When?"

"Soon." She glanced over a knee-high pile of dust and small stones that must have come from James William's room. "After what happened here, they're not going to relax until they find a new home."

I went upstairs alone. "You don't have to go up there," she called. "I was just there."

"Then I won't be disturbing them," I added.

The boxes along the hallway were higher, the paint smells from James William's room stronger. I followed the sound of a low whine to Petey's parents' room.

Petey lay on a collection of sheets and blankets on the floor by the parents' bed. A foreleg was wrapped in gauze and tape, and a special collar — one of those arrangements like an inverted lamp shade — was attached to her neck to keep her from biting the bandage.

James William lay next to her. He stroked her head, murmuring endlessly, "Good girl, you're a really good girl."

The beagle raised her head and gave me a mournful look — a combination of self-pity, pain, confusion and insistence that asked me to explain why I hadn't been here when she needed me.

The boy had a hand on the beagle's shoulder and pushed her back onto the sheets. "There's no rocks here, Petey. You don't have to worry about those big bad rocks hurting you now."

I dove through the floor and emerged from the wall with my nose inches from the spout of Gilda's coffee pot.

"Rocks! My dog got hurt by rocks?"

"Calm down. We don't know it was Fergus." Gilda's voice was firm, but she didn't trust herself enough to leave the shadows of her pot. "There was just this rock. And it hit the dog. And we don't know where it came from."

But I knew. And I was beginning to define the limits to which I'd go to deal with a Tosser.

For a while, I must have left my pot every twenty or thirty minutes to go back upstairs, and every time, Petey woke up to watch me. I'd like to think she missed me and would have come to me if I had asked her. Whatever was going on in her inquisitive beagle mind, it was disturbing her rest. So eventually, I went into my pot and stayed there, tossing and turning until nearly sunset before falling into a deep sleep.

I woke with the clear sense that something was wrong. Out of the coffee pot I shot, dove into the wall and zipped through plaster, pipes and wires to the foot of the bed in the parents' room.

The sheets were rumpled, the blanket wound into a beagle-sized nest; toys and dirty clothes were strewn across the floor. All the earmarks of a sudden departure.

"Alice!" someone screamed from the living room below. "ALICE!"

I dropped through the floor like an anchor and zoomed to the front of the house. Petey's mother and father were in the living room, putting up a brave show of courage. Laughing, slapping their thighs, making too much of their amusement. I zipped through the foyer wall, prepared to find on the other side a couple of well-armed thugs holding Petey and James William at knife point.

Crouched on the other side of the wall were a bookcase and a potted schefflera.

From the television, a dark-haired man in a jacket too tight for his belly screamed and flailed the air like a demented windmill. Petey's mother and father were guffawing their heads off, as though nothing had happened.

"What's wrong with you people?" I screamed. "Hey, there. Pay attention."

Gilda materialized at my side. "What's going on?"

"The dog is gone. And the boy, too. And these morons can't tear their empty heads from the tube."

"Well, maybe —"

I couldn't wait for the end of the sentence. If the trail wasn't too cold, I'd be able to track them.

I popped through the wall into full darkness; I'd slept several hours past my normal wake-up time. A small van trundled down the street, while, going the other direction, was an old car that left a plume of smoke hanging in the air from its tailpipe.

Neither vehicle triggered an alert in my mind: there was plenty of time for me to check both of them out. First, I had to ensure I wasn't missing a clearer, stronger trail.

Like a sparrow with a bee on its butt, I zipped around the townhouses at the water's edge. No predators lurked in the shadows, no bodies or signs of a struggle. Only a little boy playing with a dog. No vehicles lying in wait, no spent ammunition glistening on the lawn, no tire tracks burned into the road by a speeding vehicle.

Wait a minute. What was that about a boy and a dog?

James William had a heavy rope, which he threw onto the grass behind the townhouse, keeping a good hold of one end. Petey darted for the rope the instant it landed, growling and gripping it with her teeth, shaking it and backing away from James William. The boy let the beagle have her way until only a few inches remained in his hands, then he'd reel it in, with Petey snarling and fighting the entire time.

I floated directly above Petey. Part of me – okay, most of me – was disappointed to find the dog so engaged in her tussle that she wasn't aware of my presence. Whatever self-pity I had evaporated like ice cubes in the noonday desert when I saw again the bandage on Petey's leg.

Growing in transcendence, becoming more than a former breather, putting one's afterlife onto a high plane, required a commitment not so much to lofty goals, but to ennobling ways of dealing with whichever world is before us. We had to be better than we were in our first lives. And the grand reward for our spiritual betterment, it was whispered by the old-timers at our meetings, was an existence of pure love, wisdom and compassion for all of creation.

Before that happened, though, I intended to hurt someone.

Margie was pacing in front of the window in her second-story apartment. For the first time since I've known her, she was in something other than a long white gown in an 1800s style – in this case, blue jeans, and a nicely tailored white shirt accented by a paisley vest, with a blue ribbon tying her hair into a pony tail.

I knew I should have told Gilda where I was going, but the chemistry between that spook and this two-fer was too complicated to figure out. Besides, I was too fired up to risk anybody trying to talk me out of my plan.

I zipped through her neighbor's apartment – a single room shared by two male college students that smelled of unwashed everything – and circled through the hallway to the door to Margie's.

"Knock, knock," I shouted.

"Who's there?"

"Boo."

"Boo who?"

"Don't cry. I'm coming in."

I've had plenty of occasions to enter a room and be greeted by disappointment. This was the first entrance I've made during which my greeter took one look at me and nearly burst into tears.

"I thought you were Hank."

"I thought I was Hank, too. That's what a lot of head injuries as a kid can do for you."

"Where's Hank? Is he alright?"

"Hank isn't with me. He's away, doing other stuff, big stuff."

"It sounds very important."

"Hank will never admit the importance of his not being here now. What a guy."

"I'll say," she said.

I took a slow careful look around. Spooks can be anywhere, in the trash can, under a knitted scarf, between the threads of a towel drying on the radiator, or inside the wall and peering out through the holes in an electrical plate.

"What's the matter?" she asked. My guardedness must have been making her fidgety.

"I'm being sure Fergus isn't in the area."

"Don't you have some way to hide from him?"

I pointed to the over-sized bath towel draped across a radiator.

"Get that," I said. "Now hold it over your head and shoulders. Hold it up and out, so I can slip underneath." Which, true to my word, I did.

Margie, I discovered, used Jergens lotion, sweet but somehow earthy, conjuring up feelings of security and warmth and, at the end of the day, before I've snuggled under thick down quilts, freshly made chocolate chip cookies.

"Is this going to keep other spooks out?" Margie asked.

"Yeah, sure." But I wasn't sure it would protect me from the ghosts I carried. Ghosts from the other side, from my days in the sunshine. Distant memories I'd struggled to get didn't seem so important now that they were close. I wasn't sure I wanted them.

Margie said, "The reporter says the family will be there tonight to open the tomb. In about an hour. He's bringing a photographer."

I looked at Margie. Be in the present, I told myself, soak up the present; that ought to protect me from the abyss of the past. Margie's eyes were bright and intense, and I knew that was wrong. The eyes should be closed. I studied her skin: it was smooth and white. That much was right. Although it ought to be cool, too.

"Is there anything special you want me to do?" she asked.

"Yes." I wanted to close my eyes, to break this link with Margie that was bringing in half-formed thoughts and ill-remembered details from a past that was gone and buried. But much as I wanted to glance away, I was more afraid of closing my eyes and imprisoning myself in the darkness of my own mind.

"Yes," I tried again. "Once the tomb is open, brace yourself. About a dozen spooks will come flying out. You must step inside immediately after they leave. Check to make sure no one was left behind."

"I can do that."

Fantasies and phantasms, memories and terrors shuddered the foundations of my soul. I clenched my jaw. This was not the moment to lose control.

"One more thing." I spoke through gritted teeth. "Before you leave, you must check the tomb for a piece of paper. Something with writing on it. When you find it – and you will find it, because I know it's there – stuff it in a pocket. Say nothing to anyone until you've shown it to me."

Margie smiled. I could practically feel the too-warm skin, smell the lotion, sense the weight on my chest of the feather-quilt. My stomach seized. Something churned through my guts. If I wasn't careful, it would escape and ruin everything.

"Is there something else?"

"Yes, leave the tomb quickly after you have that paper."

"No, I mean something you want to tell me."

My struggle with the demon inside was over in an instant. I looked at her and said, "I miss you, Grandmother."

Twenty Eight

CHAPTER

O f all the dumb things I've said on two planes of existence, that moment with Margie was at the top of the list, with the nearest contender far, far behind. I managed to brush it aside as a joke that fizzled, although with Margie it was sometimes difficult to see the difference between a normally puzzled look and a special puzzled look.

I left her apartment through the second-floor wall and slid above the trees of Jackson Ward, numb and confused, triumphant yet beaten.

I had had a memory. A genuine, bona fide, no-bull recollection from my first life, and it told me that I had a grandmother. Who, fortunately, for all concerned, wasn't Margie. But thanks to the memories triggered by my two-fer stand-in, I know how my grandmother smelled, the bed where I slept at her house, the touch of maple that she added to her chocolate chip cookies, and I was starting to retrieve her picture from the recesses of my mind. It was barely a silhouette, but I was sure – I knew with a certainty rarely felt on this side of the Great Divide – that I would soon be able to tell you the color of her eyes, how she wore her hair, the stitched figures on her apron, the style of her favorite dress.

I did cartwheels in the air. I whooped until my breathless lungs ached. I corkscrewed upward through the clouds that blanketed the city and muted its multi-colored splendor. Perhaps I would keep going, rising until the moon became a sharply chiseled point of ice, and I would pass through the shadow thrown by the earth when the sun was on its other side, and slipping outside of that solar shield, find my astral being blasted by the full, uncloaked power of a cosmic storm.

Perhaps that was the light we were supposed to move toward, the sunshine that can nourish us or end our existence or transport us to a higher level of transcendence and the moment of judgment.

My spirit was determined to rise and keep rising until the questions slipped behind me. But I looked down, saw the blot of darkness lying on the southwestern edge of downtown Richmond, where the river glistened like a knife preparing to cut into the cemetery. And suddenly, the prospect of feeling the sun's unfiltered rays was terrifying. If that was the instant of judgment, then the verdict facing me was an unmerciful one.

For I had responsibilities waiting down there.

I glided a couple of laps over Hollywood Cemetery before I saw Fergus and a breather I didn't know. They were talking to Jedediah at his gravesite.

"What's going on?" I said, materializing on top of Jedediah's headstone.

"I was just admiring this young man's shovel," Jedediah said. If nervousness could be bottled, Jedediah was about to corner the world-market. "Isn't it just amazing how technology has changed even a simple tool?"

Technology might have changed, but not the fact that spooks can't get into their own sealed caskets.

Fergus swept the old spook with a harsh gaze. "Ain't it also amazing to find out Blackbeard's pirate treasure is buried in this actual grave. What are the odds of that happening?"

Jedediah trembled and lost focus. I saw the lights of the city through his hazy figure.

"I . . . I . . . can't rightly say," he said.

"I'd say the odds were – let me see." Fergus's finger stabbed the air as though operating an invisible pocket calculator. "– approximately zero."

"I was just thinking," Jedediah muttered. "Since you're here and all. With that nice shovel."

In the silence that followed, you could practically hear a just-expired candle wick moan.

"Isn't that old poem going to be worth just as much to you as Blackbeard's treasure?" I worked a spectral, hand-cranked adding machine in the air. "Which is to say – nothing."

Fergus gave me the evil eye. "I promised Ramona that I'd get her that scrap of paper, if it's the last thing I do."

"I hate to break this to you," I said cheerfully, "but you've already done your last thing."

"Not yet."

I had to give him some credit. "This is a point of honor for you."

"Yeah. And don't expect me to play nicey-nice."

"Well, I won't stand in your way."

Technically, my response passed the moral scrub test: I didn't intend to stop him from getting into that tomb, although I did intend an improvisation or two that I hadn't mentioned to Fergus.

Throughout this, Fergus's friend's head went from one of us to the other, like an umpire in a ping-pong contest.

"Who's the two-fer?" I asked.

"This is Rawley, and he's no two-fer." Fergus leaned toward me; his eyes reminded me of a dying swamp. "He thinks he's having a reaction to some very serious drugs."

Rawley snapped out of his trance momentarily, but I realized I was dangerously close to slipping into a world of my own, too. How did my moral code compare to Fergus's? If there was a difference, was it big enough for anyone to notice? Or care about?

I needed a meeting. Or Cal. Or another spook to talk this over with.

Jedediah gazed at me with a rare trace of expectancy. He had been standing watch at this old gravesite before the birth of my grandmother who made cookies into a food fit for godlings. Did a tomb-squatter have any advice for a specter in recovery, other than the suggestion that you ought to go outside some bright afternoon if you find yourself seriously entertaining the idea of hunting for your own grave?

Turns out, Jedediah did. Was that slyness that flickered across his face? Was the old boy really capable of insight into transcendence? I don't know for sure, but there was no uncertainty about his advice:

"A spook's got to do what a spook's got to do," he told me.

"Then let's do it," I answered.

I took Fergus and Rawley around the next hill from Jedediah's grave. We went at a breather's pace and I used the time to lay out my plan for getting into the mausoleum.

We could see shadows of breathers moving in front of the tombs. The homes that surround the cemetery had mostly shut down for the night; in the city beyond, the air was filled with the unsleeping hum of a metropolis.

Word had gotten out in the recovery community that something special was going to happen here tonight, and the trees of the cemetery were decorated with spooks sitting, reclining, hanging and otherwise loitering in hopes of seeing a show.

"You only get one chance to mess this up," I told Fergus. "This has got to come off like a well-oiled machine. And you're the most likely screw to come loose. No second chances."

"You're a helpful guy, Mr. Ralph. You care about your fellow specters." Fergus was the only spook I've ever run across who can glide with a swagger. "I'm sure if we run into some difficulty, we'll persuade you to have a repeat."

I fixed Fergus was a stare that I hoped, after a few years practice, would someday kill athlete's foot. "One chance. No repeats. No foul ups."

"Okay, okay," Fergus said.

This was a moment when you either press your advantage or slide back into the honey bucket. I pressed.

"Again," I said, "run through the plan."

"Jeez, this is so lame." Fergus whined. I shot him a look. He straightened up and said, "The family opens the tomb. We give the idiot spooks inside some time to leave. I figure about three-quarters of a second will be enough. Then my boy Rawley, pretending he's with the cemetery, goes inside. He needs to make sure the tomb is safe for breathers, we say. He grabs the paper and skedaddles. He's halfway to Philadelphia before anyone realizes they aren't going to find any gems of literature in there."

Fergus picked up a pebble and flicked it into a bush. Two spooks scurried for the high branches. "One thing I don't understand. What's to stop someone from going inside before Rawley."

"Who's going to try?" I asked.

Of course, among my candidates were Margie, the reporter Briscow, a newspaper photographer, a few representatives of the Squires family and a couple of genuine grounds-keepers from the cemetery.

I watched a platoon of rebel spooks glide in formation into the upper branches of a massive oak. One of them carried a homemade pennant with the stitched message: *Never Say Die!*

For a while, a Confederate spook named Ben was a regular at our nightly 12-step meeting. Ben spoke candidly about his suspicions about recovery programs, seeing as how the granddaddy of all meetings, Alcoholics Anonymous, was founded in Akron, Ohio, practically the heart of the Yankee beast.

Anyway, Ben liked to couch his remarks in military metaphors. I remember him saying that the first casualty of every battle was the plan the generals had concocted for waging the battle. That little piece of wisdom played through my mind as I scooted toward the tomb, followed by Fergus and his breather, Rawley.

I settled down next to Margie. "Rub your nose for *Yes* and your chin for *No*."

"Why would I want to do that?" she asked.

"So the reporter and the photographer don't see you talking to yourself and think you're completely insane."

"Ah," she said. Then rubbed her nose. *Yes.*

"As soon as the door is open, you're going inside, getting the paper and hiding it in your clothing."

Nose rub. *Yes.*

"And are you going to let anyone – breather, spook or anything in between – stop you?"

Chin rub. *No.*

Behind me, I heard a tinkling noise that reminded me of a line from Edgar Allan: *the tintinabulation of the bells.* I think I've always liked that word. *Tintinabulation.* I'm now into my second life and still waiting for the chance to work it into a conversation.

I glanced back. The reporter Briscow, jingling a key ring, shuffled toward the bronze doors of the mausoleum, followed by a young woman with several large-lensed cameras hanging from her neck.

Behind them, Fast Eddie waited (for once) exactly where I asked him to be. And behind him, several breathers were shielded by layers of darkness under the trees. Folks from the cemetery, I thought, and more members of the Squires family.

"Why'd you let Fergus come here?" Margie hissed. "He's going to make trouble."

"The only way he'll believe the poem isn't inside, is if he's here when the mausoleum opens."

"But he'll find out we've taken the poem. I mean, isn't that the point? To tell the world in tomorrow's newspaper that we found a new poem by Edgar Allan Poe."

"Yeah, well, when that happens, I hope we'll have him settled down and under control."

Margie scowled. "What's your backup plan?"

"I hear they've got good meetings at the North Pole."

Briscow jiggled the key into the lock, then turned the key. A flash tore through the darkness as his photographer snapped a picture of the great event.

From the corner of my eye, I saw Fergus's breather, Rawley, begin moving forward. Fergus, in a rare recognition of normal human reactions, stayed back, distancing himself from responsibility for anything his puppet was about to do.

The puppet, which is to say, Rawley, had covered about half the distance to the mausoleum when the bronze doors swung open slightly. And a mass of raging spectral energy came boiling out into the night, spooks so pissed off, eager to escape, and fired up to sweep away any last-second impediments, that nothing short of a thermonuclear device was going to get their attention.

The breathers, of course, didn't see any of this. Nor did they notice Fast Eddie sidling up to Rawley and letting loose about twenty coffee beans. When Hank and I concocted this plan, I was concerned we'd have to come up with a buzzing sound that Rawley could hear in order for this trick to work. Once Fast Eddie got the coffee beans swirling in front of Rawley's face and bumping into the man's forehead and cheeks every now and then, we didn't need a soundtrack for the goon to think he had run into a nest of killer bees.

"Aaaaiiiiyyyee!" Rawley squealed. He punched and slapped his face, swinging like a madman at tiny shadows, before locking his forearm over his eyes and running across the road.

While everyone was watching Rawley, Margie walked inside. I'm sure not even Briscow saw her enter.

The young reporter was – to use an unfortunate phrase – spooked by Rawley's bizarre behavior. Instinctively, he pulled the doors shut. I saw him turn the key so the bolt would slide back into place. Rebel Ben's insight into fouled up plans came back to me like a blast of sunshine. If Briscow locked Margie inside, would he notice? If not, how could I get word to him? Or would he show a dark side and leave the woman trapped there?

A strange chorus of voices began chanting from the trees.

"Twenty for a head shot."

"You're on."

"Five for the belly."

"I got you there."

"A miss. I got thirty-five says Henderson doesn't lay an inch of wood on him."

"I want a piece of that."

"Yo, in the trees. Me, too."

"Fifty says he hits him somewhere."

Specters squatting in the trees and perched on headstones were laying odds about what would happen when Rawley staggered off the road, into a row of headstones and, all unknowing, entered Henderson's strike zone. The tomb-squatter gripped a spectral bat and took a firm stance in the far left corner of his gravesite, waiting for the moron to bumble, weave and meander within range.

It was a fascinating drama, even for the spooks who were aware that the worst Henderson could do was to send a chilly shiver through Rawley if he clipped him with the bat.

I was no exception to the ghostly horde riveted upon Henderson's gently swaying bat and Rawley's blind, clomping approach. Looking back, I'm pretty sure it was about that time I heard knuckles faintly rapping, rapping on a chamber door.

Rawley was coming hot down the center of Henderson's strike zone. It was looking like he'd split the plate. Henderson was as cool as a chilled cucumber. The screams of the fans couldn't make that spook take his eyes off his encounter with destiny.

A strange creaking and scrapping came from the tomb. I turned. The bronze doors were open, Briscow's hand on the handle, and Margie had just stepped outside. A wry smile played upon her lips.

Then hell, quite literally, burst loose. A wave of light crashed against the front of the mausoleum, searing, boiling, pummeling the existence out of anything ill-fated and spectral enough to stray into the beam. Margie and Briscow raised their hands to protect themselves from the light. From trees and car roofs and the tops of headstones and statues, a hundred or more spooks *poofed* away to different continents.

I darted behind a tree and, when I was confident the light wasn't seeking me in particular, peered around the trunk.

The breathers I'd seen earlier by the tomb included Margie's friends from Hollywood, the movie capital, that is, recording for posterity the great moment when their little understudy became the savior of western literature.

Margie, approaching the cameras, caught my eye and winked.

I was about to wink back when Hank, who must have been the only spook beside myself to hold his ground, said, simply, "Where'd Fergus go?"

Twenty Nine
CHAPTER

ext evening, sitting in the back booth of the diner, the fear and euphoria of that moment still set the old ectoplasm percolating. Fast Eddie wasn't eager to tell his friends in recovery that he'd taken a dangerous step toward the bright side by manipulating physical objects, even something as innocent as coffee beans, and for such a good cause. But that didn't stop him from telling each new arrival about the killer bees that showed up at just the moment when he started to think we needed a few little pricks.

Rosetta's capacity for laughter dried up in the presence of *a single-entendre*. She suggested that *stinger* would be a more appropriate name for the weapons of the Apidae family, although she appreciated the humor of Fergus's exit.

"I'm sure the poor fellow will find true companionship among the rats and spiders," she said.

"What have you got against rats and spiders?" Gilda asked.

For the next fifteen seconds, Gilda and I were the only spooks in the booth who didn't consider a shaker of sugar the most fascinating thing we'd seen in this life.

I don't know where Gilda had found a bucket yesterday to spend the daylight hours. All signs were that Petey and her family would be moving elsewhere by the weekend, and I'd have to find a new home, too. Meanwhile, a moment of reckoning was coming with Gilda for not including her in the hoopla last night at the Squires mausoleum.

Rosetta leaned across the table. My grandmother, I was coming to remember, wore steel-rimmed glasses like hers. Perhaps Rosetta sensed something new in my attitude toward her — a softening, an opening, an interest — because the way she treated me had changed. And I'm not entirely sure it was for the better.

"You can't hold yourself accountable for what happened to Fergus," she said. "He went into that tomb under his own power and to satisfy his own greed. He knew how dangerous it is for a spook to invade the burial grounds of another."

"But he didn't know that reporter was going to close the tomb at that moment," I shot back. "Or that the lights from the movie cameras would block his only way out."

"Nobody said death is fair," Rosetta said.

Cal rubbed his thick hand across his eyes. The little group of spooks grew still. Tablets were going to be handed down from the mountain.

"Fergus dug his own grave," Cal said. "Now he's going to have to sleep in it."

Our usual meeting-before-the-meeting ended about an hour before the start of our regular meeting and about two hours before our meeting-after-the-meeting. A few spooks at the diner left to talk to their sponsors. Some went to check the gutters and alleys downtown for newbies. Others wanted to catch the nightly parade above Monument Avenue.

I headed for the cemetery. I might not be able to get Fergus out, but maybe that Tosser had rethought his attitude about transcendence, seeing as how his amusements for the indefinite future are going to consist of the comings and goings of various insects.

Henderson had already finished the nightly inspection of his gravesite, and he stood on top of his headstone when I arrived, twirling his bat as if it were a cheerleader's baton.

"Did you see it?" he said. "That ball was bobbing and weaving like a cork on the ocean. It could have broken to the left or to the right. It could have popped up or dove into the dust. Heck, it could have turned around and gone back. But I nailed it, hard and square."

"That was no ball, Henderson. That was a breather."

"Yeah, well, look how much harder that is. A baseball's only got the law of physics to determine where it's going. A breather's got free will."

I didn't have the heart to tell Henderson I was distracted and didn't actually see his great moment with Rawley and the swarm of killer coffee beans.

"You've got a good swing," I said.

"Good? That was the stuff of folk songs."

"Yeah."

Drifting across the road to the Squires mausoleum, I felt the thermometer plummet. Funny how the chill of the cemetery hadn't been so noticeable the last couple of nights when spooks were in trouble here. I wonder if the change was sensed by the regulars like Henderson, Jedediah and the other tomb-squatters who chose to make a dead-end of their afterlives.

Either frost was forming on the bronze doors of the tomb, or Fergus's personality was hastening their decay. I couldn't tell.

Careful not to get too close to the doors and hopeful that Fergus was in some other part of the tomb (*Okay, I wasn't thinking clearly. Where could he have gone? The wine-cellar? The indoor swimming pool? The attached, four-broomstick garage?*), I whispered, "You in there, Fergus?"

"WHERE DO YOU THINK I AM, YOU ECTOPLASMIC NITWIT?"

"I was wondering if you wanted to talk, to get your feelings out."

"The thing I want to get out isn't my feelings. And talking isn't what I had in mind."

"Let me share with you my personal experiences with *thanks-a-bunch* moments –"

"Oh, goody," Fergus snarled. "Then I get to share the personal experiences I hope to have with your scrawny, worthless neck."

"You know, technically, even if you were on this side of the door, my neck isn't going to be in any danger."

"What are you willing to bet on it, spook-face?"

It's not much of an infinite universe, Rosetta likes to say, *if we know what's around every corner.* Which I've not found to be one of the program's most comforting ideas.

"Well," I said. "This has been a good beginning. Thanks for sharing that, Fergus."

Backing away from the bronze doors, I gave my friendliest wave, while the door answered back with an arctic gust that rattled the hinges and strained the lock.

Gilda was waiting behind me.

"I'd say that was very encouraging," she said. "I can see Fergus getting paroled for good behavior within the life of this star system."

"There's always hope."

"Hmmm," she replied.

Gilda may be a spook, but she's still capable of putting more layers of meaning around a murmur than I care to unwrap.

"About the other night —" I started.

"You were moving fast," she said. "I understand."

Was I actually on the verge of hugging a Goth? Would I be laughed out of the here-after for merely thinking such an absurd idea? Could I forgive myself if I tried?

Before I could wander far down that path, Gilda said, "So, no more loose ends flapping in the wind?"

I cupped a hand over an ear. "Can't hear any."

"Let me help."

Gilda grabbed me by the astral shirt collar and *(poof)* took me away.

There was something familiar about the wooden door that appeared inches from my rematerialized nose. Glancing to either side, I saw a hallway with bad lighting, poor wallpaper and worse carpeting.

I may be a spook, who's still recovering from a lifetime spent flooded with testosterone, but the little sparks that began flying through my head were too much to ignore. This was Margie's apartment building.

"You want to bring me here?" I asked.

"Loose end," Gilda said and pointed to the door. She adjusted the lapels of her black leather coat and, to herself, added: "My money's on some spook getting slapped in the face for a few more decades by that loose end."

Poof.

Gone was the need for me to figure out whether I should thank Gilda for bringing me here or to wonder if this was the perfect moment to check on the Specters Anonymous program in Rangoon.

But, since I'd come all this way, wouldn't it be silly to leave without paying a visit?

"Knock, knock," I shouted.

"Who's there?"

"Hatch."

"Hatch who?"

"Bless you. Now, may I come in?"

Margie sat in the middle of her apartment floor, surrounded by a dozen opened newspapers. She was beaming.

"Did you see the story?"

"Somebody left a paper in the diner, turned to that page. We all were able to read it."

Local Psychic Finds Earliest Poe Writing, the headline read. Printed alongside a lengthy article bylined C. A. Briscow was a photograph of Margie emerging from the mausoleum. Her expression in the photo was unusual, a mixture of pleasure and perplexity. Of course, the caption writer didn't know that, at the instant the photo was taken, Fergus was zipping through Margie's skull.

"The reason you wanted me to hide that poem in my pocket when I left," she said, her focus now turned to her television screen and the remote control in her hand, "was because of the spook who went in the tomb as I was leaving."

"That's it."

"He's alright?"

I gave the question some serious thought. "He's probably better than he's been in a long time."

"Good." Margie went back to her remote control. "Have you seen this?"

With the punch of a button, I could see Margie on the screen being interviewed by the local ABC affiliate, then the CBS and NBC stations, then CNN's headline news. The Christian Broadcasting Corporation story carried the headline, *A God-Sent Message from Beyond*, while FOX labeled it, *Anti-Religion Hoax in Richmond*.

"You sure got a lot of coverage in the papers," I mused.

Local Psychic Finds Earliest Poe Writing read the headline in each of the dozen papers strewn across the floor. I drifted over for a closer look. They were all today's edition of the Richmond paper.

"I can see why you'd want extra copies of the paper," I said, "but why open every one to the same page?"

"I wanted to make sure the story was still there."

I was coming to recognize the limits of a special place called Margie-Land, where specterhood can seem pretty humdrum.

"With the publicity you're getting, you'll be up to your ears in customers once you hang out your shingle," I said.

Margie was confused. "Why would I hang shingles? I want to be a spiritual advisor, not a roofer."

"Doesn't hurt to have a back-up plan."

Rosetta convened the nightly meeting of the St. Sears group of Specters Anonymous. The eye contact between her and Cal beforehand had been a little, well, spooky, so I wasn't surprised when she announced that one of our oldest members had asked to lead the meeting.

"Name's Cal," he said. "I'm a grateful spook. And I want to talk about sunshine."

Hank crossed his legs, getting comfortable, preparing to hear sacred script interpreted by a master. Rosetta, who had a few decades of recovery on Cal, put on a peculiar smile that I associate with finding a slice of lime hidden in a salad. Gilda checked her nails. The newbies leaned closer, drawn to the quiet authority of Cal's voice.

"Strange to admit now, but there was a time I couldn't imagine stringing two nights together without a spot of sunshine between them. Now, I can't imagine actually having that bright stuff touch me.

"Like I said, I'm a spook, and I want you to hear me plainly. The afterlife isn't something that I'm going through. That I'm trying to endure. That was imposed on me.

"Being a spook is what I choose for myself. One night at a time. And I simply won't put up with having it any other way."

His eyes swept the room. I knew what was coming.

"Ralph," he said. "It would do my transcendence good to hear you talk about sunshine. What does it mean to you? How do you deal with it? Do you want to go back?"

I straightened in my chair. "Ralph here. I'm a spook. And, sure, I want to go back. A lot sometimes, and a little bit more often. I don't think I'd be a real spook if part of me didn't want to hang around old houses and go *BOO* at the breathers."

That last bit, said with feeling and appropriate gestures, always got a laugh. Cal looked nervous. Anything that makes the old specter a little uneasy is a good thing in my book.

"I'm not sure about the transcendence part of the program," I went on. "Can I talk myself into being transcendent? I don't think so. But, after coming to these meetings for a few nights – and seeing what happens to spooks who think they can still play in the sunshine – I know that when it comes to daylight, I'm utterly incompetent to dabble in that sandbox."

If Cal had been a breather, I believe he would have let out a great sigh. Rosetta seemed to find a personal sense of accomplishment that I hadn't used the words *carcass, road kill, worm food* or *daisy fertilizer.*

Before a proper silence could descend over the group, Fast Eddie said he wanted to share and took about ten minutes talking about the fun he used to have in his first life, sitting on the beach for days at a time, until his skin was redder than an autumn sunset and when he closed his eyelids, he could still see the sun firing up the sky.

For the rest of the meeting, the conversation drifted along familiar paths. Spooks in crisis, spooks okay, spooks who didn't want to be there, spooks who didn't seem to understand where they were but still wanted to talk about it.

As we were breaking up, I gave Cal an atta-boy thumbs-up for a meeting well led. He pointed at me and said from across the room, "What are you doing tonight to help the still-suffering spook?"

"I know, I know."

On the stoop, Rosetta was trying to congratulate Hank for cleaning up his vocabulary. Hank kept thanking her for her kindness but was incapable of not sprinkling each sentence with a few choice words about the *crispy critters* and *charcoal brickheads* who came here through cremation.

Standing to one side of the stairs leading to the sidewalk was Margie.

"I didn't want to disturb your meeting," she said. "But I meant to tell you something earlier."

"What?"

"That maybe you should come by some night. I enjoy watching DVDs, especially old television shows. In fact, I was planning to pick up *The Honeymooners* from the library tomorrow."

"*The Honeymooners*, huh? Now, where'd you get the idea that I'd be interested in that?"

Margie put her hands behind her back and swung her hips very prettily. She had a smile that would convince a tomb-squatter to take a stroll.

"A little birdie told me," she said.

Just then, Gilda passed us on the steps. "Tweet, tweet," she said, then she *poofed*.

CHAPTER Thirty

Untitled poem by Edgar Allan Poe. Earliest extant example of the author's work, written at approximately 13 years of age. *Poe: Poetry and Tales* (New York: Library of America, 2012), p. 103.

Mary had a little lamb
Whose fleece was black as coal,
And everywhere that Mary went
The lamb was sure to ~~roll~~.

> ~~toll~~
> ~~bowl~~
> ~~enroll~~
> ~~scroll~~
> ~~cajole~~
> ~~make like a mole~~
> ~~talk en Espanol~~
> [illegible]

—The End—

A Preview follows of
The first chapter from Phil Budahn's latest novel
About Specters Anonymous

Nelle, Nook & Randall

Available on Kindle and at Amazon.Com
Beginning April 1, 2013

Note to self: That's April Fool's Day.
You can remember that, can't you?

Nelle, Nook & Randall
By Phil Budahn
Chapter One

It started with fireflies. Flickering in a mayonnaise jar, sending beads of greenish-yellow light into the darkness. Gilda squatted on the porch of our duplex, her nose inches from the glass.

"They're avoiding each other," she said. "Each one's as far as he can get from the others."

I checked the blinking dots of light. "What do you expect? Five or six born leaders in there, and not a single born follower."

She shot me a look that died quicker than a firefly's spark, then turned back to the jar. "I thought insects worked those things out. You know, queens and drones —"

"— hierarchies and lowerarchies," I added.

"— a place for everyone."

"Put yourself behind their antennas," I said. "If you were a firefly, who would you pick to follow? Every wanna-be leader in there is an idiot who'd keep you awake with the light flashing from his backside."

Gilda pursed her lips. The greenish-yellow glow of the fireflies sank into her black leather jacket without a trace. Nor did they have the briefest glimmer on her cheeks, although bright specks ricocheted from the leaves of the honey-suckle below the porch.

"What do you think would happen if I put my hand in the jar?" she asked. "Will I get all itchy and woozy? Will I start dissolving into nothingness?"

"More likely, the fireflies will find a way to get out," I answered.

She lifted a hand, her purple fingernails seemed to brush the glossy glass surface, and the fireflies darted to the bottom of the container and formed a swirling, twinkling, lime-yellow bundle. No concerns now in insect world about who was in charge.

"Hey," I said. "They can see you."

"So, will they attack me if my hand is inside?" Gilda's eyes gleamed, her fingers thrummed near the jar. "Will they fry my vital essence with the power of their lights? Will I be blasted into more pieces of ectoplasm than can ever be reassembled? Will my essence go twirling into the bottomless abyss?"

"One way to find out," I said. "Stick your arm in there."

Okay, maybe I wasn't making a serious suggestion. Maybe I didn't think central Virginia's most devout Goth would stoop to do anything on my say-so. Or maybe I should have remembered that somewhere beneath Gilda's eye-liner and mascara a couple truckloads of indignation balanced on a hair-trigger.

"You'd let me do that, wouldn't you?" Her eyes bored into me. "You'd actually stand there and say nothing while I plunged by fingers into a jar of light."

"We're talking fireflies," I protested. "There's not a single healthy photon coming from the bunch of them."

Gilda's eyes gave off a black heat. "Some mentor you are," she said and left in a righteous *poof.*

Welcome to another night in the here-after.

If having a heartbeat was such a good idea, you wouldn't be on the dark side of the daisies now, according to Cal.

I've always suspected there was a flaw in his logic, but whenever I try to pry it out, I get a headache.

Besides, it doesn't matter whether the advice makes sense. Cal is my sponsor in the 12-step recovery program of Specters Anonymous. He gets to run my afterlife. He also can tell me to stop talking, sit up straight and quit fidgeting.

I, on the other hand, don't get to tell anyone anything. Especially not myself. And in the rare eventuality that some night the seas would part, flotillas of flying carpets would land at JFK International Airport and Cal would let me serve as some other spook's sponsor, I will neither volunteer for, nor accept under duress, nor find a suitable bribe to take responsibility for Gilda.

One train wreck in my afterlife is enough. Thank you, very much. I'm my own accident-in-progress.

On this particular night, by the time I left the porch of our duplex a downpour began to pummel the empty streets of Richmond, punctuated by an occasional blast of lightning and a drum-roll of thunder. My home meeting, the St. Sears group, had already started when I floated through the basement door of the old church on the north side of Church Hill.

Gilda managed to glare at me without actually looking in my direction, although an empty gray metal chair next to her began to exert a tidal pull. I gritted my teeth and, smiling at Mrs. Hannity and Darleen, nodding to Roger and

Fast Eddie, wishing good evening to a few chairs that didn't, technically, have occupants at the moment, I struggled into a seat beside Hank.

He leaned over. "Gilda is putty in your hands. Everyone here can see that."

Hank has a *cafe au lait* complexion, a pig-tail at the back of his head and more residual testosterone than anyone knows what to do with on this side of the Great Divide.

I gazed about the room; most of the regulars were here, plus a sprinkling of newbies. The newcomers were easy to pick out: they were the ones actually listening to Fast Eddie talk about the swarm of killer bees that once descended on a city cemetery at the decisive moment to permit the escape of a couple hundred poor souls trapped in a stranger's tomb.

Among the details Fast Eddie edited out of his yarn (details being an impediment to the narrative flow) were the facts that only eight spooks had been trapped; killer bees were nowhere in sight, although reliable reports said flying coffee beans plagued one of the bad guys; and the coffee beans weren't airborne because of a deity but through Fast Eddie's secret skill at levitation.

My attention snapped back online as Fast Eddie concluded, "And that's my story, and I'm sticking to it."

"Thank you for sharing your *perplexities, tremors and fantasies*," said our leader, Rosetta, using one of the zippier phrases from our literature. "Who'd like to share next?"

Gilda flicked up a hand with purple fingernails barely poking beyond the cuff of her jacket. Gilda usually let her black leather and chains do the talking for her, so the simple gesture raised eyebrows among the St. Sears regulars.

"Gilda here. And I'm an old-fashioned specter," she said. "I like going to sleep before dawn and waking up at sunset. There are never too many shadows for me. Going down the street and being able to step right through people – I still can't figure out whether I want to puke or feel like I've died and gone to heaven."

Hearing one of the *H* words, Rosetta straightened on her chair. If it were anyone except Gilda, I'd expect Rosetta to get fussy about inappropriate language. Since my recovery program accepts members from all spectral persuasions, we don't want to be unwelcoming to the occasional atheist, druid or zoroastrian.

Gilda had already broken her personal record for most consecutive syllables in a single evening, but she still hadn't picked the scab off whatever was bothering her. I suspected it might involve fireflies or wise-mouthed friends.

"Sometimes"– and here Gilda's eyes got a far-away expression, although that could have been her eye-liner undergoing a tectonic shift –"sometimes I wonder if I might look back some night and think that, maybe, I should let myself go. Become a rebel."

Most eyes in the room doubled in size. Gilda, our resident Goth, who drifted above the gray metal chair clad totally in black, except for the purple fingernail polish, the facial powder that glowed in the dim light and the bright red lipstick, thought she was too restrained?

Gilda lowered her voice. "I wonder if we should be doing more than talking to each other about what we think is going on. Maybe there's someone out there who has the answers. Maybe we should find her."

At that instant, a thunderclap rattled the foundations of Richmond, lights flickered, and when the illumination returned, one of the empty chairs in the back row had become a formerly empty chair.

The new arrival wore a three-piece suit, a fancy white shirt, and a tie barely wider than my thumb. His dark hair was slicked along the sides of his head and managed a peculiar wave-like construction at the top of his forehead. His smile was wide and frozen, his eyes narrow and dead.

"Madame Leader, if I may?" he told Rosetta. "Brother Randall here. And I'm the dumbest specter on two planes of existence." Something close to a collective sigh rose from the specters of a previously female disposition. I don't know about Hank or Cal or the rest of the guys, but I couldn't take my eyes from the top of Randall's head. Was it hair or a very shiny black helmet?

"I just happened to be passing by this wonderful meeting," he said. "I heard the heart-felt sharing that rose like incense from your devout members. And I wondered if I may be allowed to pass along an observation I once heard from a man far wiser than myself. Words that have meant so much to my recovery from the evils of sunshine."

Randall sopped up the attention like a dehydrated sponge. His squinty eyes probed the faces in the room. When those eyes settled on me, I felt a cold wind. Brother Randall's look slithered over to Hank and then to Mrs. Hannity. Only Cal kept his gaze level.

"That message is this—You're either digging your way out of your grave, or you're digging your way further into it. There's no status-quo here in the second life. We may be dead, but that doesn't allow us to lie around and do nothing."

Brother Randall's glance rolled over the group again with a triumphant glimmer. Except for Cal, most of the spooks were leaning forward, their eyes gleaming. Gilda stared with an expression I'd never seen before. Probably because it didn't involve anger or annoyance with me.

"I appreciate your kindness," Randall told the group. "And I look forward to hearing more about your recoveries from the terrible — and utterly false — temptations of living."

The narrow eyes that darted over the group kept darting and the smile that hadn't changed on Brother Randall's face continued not to change. Almost primly, he clasped his hands on his lap and slumped back on the metal chair.

The silence that usually settles on our meetings wasn't in evidence for the rest of the session. Newbies, who last night were fully preoccupied with looking cool and not drifting into each other, couldn't get recognized fast enough by Rosetta.

"Where have you been all my afterlife?" said one newcomer who was so far from figuring out how things worked in happily-ever-after that he had car keys hooked to a belt loop.

Half-time is an honored tradition for 12-step meetings on both sides of the Great Divide. For those of us with an aptitude for holding our breaths, there isn't much we can do except go outside for a couple minutes until the meeting resumes.

Hank had already drifted to the steps when I got there. The rain slanted through his spectral body; at any second, I expected to see droplets bouncing off the small ponytail at the back of his head.

"That spook sure knows how to raise the dead," Hank said.

"I don't know," was my best answer at the moment. I envied Brother Randall's confidence and vitality (*Note to self: Are we allowed vitality in the afterlife?*). But there was something about him that reminded me of the night I stepped in front of a searchlight and felt my ectoplasm getting blasted into cosmic dust.

"They're called *Spiritists*." Cal materialized on the edge of the sidewalk. "Most of them want to sink deep roots into this second life. Burrow in, get comfy, give this existence 100 percent of all they've got. Even forget about our first lives or the breathers around us."

"Isn't that the point of recovery?" Hank asked.

Cal shook his head.

Realizing I hadn't jammed my foot into my mouth all evening, I joined in: "You've been telling us that we've got to quit thinking that we can return to the sunshine. Isn't that what Brother Randall is saying?"

"Randall wants to settle down here," Cal answered, "but I'm just passing through. I don't want to get comfortable. Some night, I hope to balance the books for whatever caused me to be sidetracked here. There'll be a *bing* and my sorry little attitude will reappear among a better class of spooks."

"We like you, too, Cal," I said.

Cal has never been accused of touchy-feely-ism. In fact, his theory of recovery tends toward the break-bricks-and-kick-butt school. But beneath that gruff, frosty exterior is a gruff interior that's merely chilled.

He and Hank went back to the meeting. I hesitated a moment to watch a line of lightning uncoil along the western sky, thought of Gilda's fireflies and wondered if she were really worried that the minuscule wattage produced by the bugs could endanger her transcendence. How could she possibly be frightened of fireflies? As I was heading back inside, I heard *clickety-clickety-clickety* on the slate footpath at the side of the old church and knew exactly what that meant.

Darting through the corner of the church, I tried to force my ectoplasmic heart to slow down. Petey couldn't possibly be here. The weather was terrible, home was a good ten minutes away, and she wasn't supposed to be out by herself.

As I emerged from the mortar and brick, I spotted an unmistakable package of fur, flailing tongue and eyes the color of hot chocolate.

"Petey," I cried. "What are you doing here, girl? You should be home."

Petey saw through my phony toughness and was about to go up on her hind legs to lick my face when she prudently slid to a halt and stood in the downpour; her tail worked back and forth with enough energy to topple her onto her side if she weren't careful.

I squatted and, cupping my hands around her shoulders proceeded to give the beagle a good astral rub-down that went from her pudgy neck to the base of her expressive tail, all the while keeping my fingers a couple inches from the wet fur.

Dogs and cats can sense the presence of spooks in a vague, hit-or-miss way. Petey was remarkable for two reasons. First, she was able to see us directly. And second, she liked me.

Petey reacted to my astral cuddling as though it were the real deal. Guess I'll never know whether to put that down to some spiritual connection or a desire to please that ought to qualify her for another 12-step program.

"Let's get you out of the rain, sweetie," I said.

I glided to the base of the church wall, where overhanging eaves protected a narrow stretch of grass and pine needles. Petey shook out her fur, then settled on the ground. I drifted feet-first into the earth until my nose was nearly touching the beagle's.

"Now that that's taken care of," I told the wise, questioning eyes, "can you please tell me exactly what you're doing here?"

A bolt of lightning flashed, a thunderclap shook the ground, Petey shot to her feet.

"Easy, girl. I'm not going to let that big bad storm harm you."

Petey had other ideas. She leaned on her back legs and placed her front paws on the coarse brick wall, and I was certain I was about to see a beagle walk up the side of a building.

Or answer the call to the canine afterlife.

-End of Sample Chapter-

27614259R00116

Made in the USA
Charleston, SC
15 March 2014